HAVE YOU SEEN A RED CURTAIN IN MY WEARY CHAMBER?

Poems, Stories and Essays

by

Tomás Borge Martínez

with an introduction,
translation and notes by
Russell Bartley, Kent Johnson,
and Sylvia Yoneda

CURBSTONE PRESS

Acknowledgements:

Joseph Napora and Eunice Wagner offered generous solidarity in raising funds for visits by the translators to Managua; Margaret Randall and Deborah Elzinga have been sources of encouragement and inspiration from the start. All four have helped to bring this book into being, and we extend our sincere thanks to them.

— The Translators

Cover design by Barbara Byers
Printed in the U.S. by BookCrafters

This publication was supported in part by donations from private individuals and by grants from The National Endowment for the Arts and The Connecticut Commission on the Arts, a state agency whose funds are recommended by the Governor and appropriated by the State Legislature.

ISBN: 0-915306-81-6
Library of Congress number: 88-43573

Distributed in the U.S. by:
The Talman Company
150 Fifth Avenue
New York, NY 10011

Curbstone Press, 321 Jackson Street, Willimantic, CT 06226

CONTENTS

CREATIVITY IN THE REVOLUTION: THE LITERARY BORGE. By Way of an Introduction 9

WE'RE A COUNTRY OF OPEN WINDOWS
A Conversation with Tomás Borge Martínez 19

STORY NUMBER TWO 27

CLANDESTINE POEMS AND PROSE:
Clandestine Poems and Prose: Critical Comments
by Carlos Martínez Rivas 35

Hay una muchacha 40
There's a girl 41

Voy a morir bajo la lluvia 42
I'm going to die in the rain 43

De Sal y Agua 44
Of Salt and Water 45

Aurora 46
Aurora 47

En Cuatro Tiempos 48
In Four Movements 49

En Fin 50
In Sum 51

PROSE 52

FROM THE MODEL PRISON 56

LETTER TO ANA JOSEFINA 65

PRISON POEMS AND OTHER POETRY

La Ceremonia Esperada 68
The Awaited Ceremony 69

Encuentro 70
Encounter 71

Casi Todo 72
Almost Everything 73

¿Qué Harás? 74
What Are You Doing Now? 75

La Que Mastica Sueños 76
The Girl Who Chews Up Dreams 77

Nicaragua 78
Nicaragua 79

Ya No 80
No More 81

A Propósito de un Lenguaje Irrespetuoso 82
Apropos of Disrespectful Speech 83

A Propósito del Discurso de un Diputado Somocista 84
Apropos of a Speech by a Somocista Congressman 85

La Piedra 86
The Stone 87

Cumpleaños 88
Birthday 89

La Salida del Sol 90
Sunrise 91

Cuando No Estás 92
When You're Not Here 93

Nacimiento 94
Birth 95

Lámpara 96
Lamp 97

Visita en la Cárcel 98
Jail Visit 99

Verano 100
Summer 101

La Instantánea 102
Snapshot 103

Me Entregaste un Golpe de Ruiseñor 104
You Gave Me the Jolt of a Nightingale 105

Represión 106
Repression 107

No Estoy 112
I Am Not 113

Lo Tuyo, Lo Mío 114
Yours, Mine 115

Ahí Estaba 116
There It Was 117

Che 118
Che 119

La Dulce Condición 122
The Gentle Condition 123

THE STORY OF MACHO MALO 131

THE REBIRTH OF JOSE CORONEL URTECHO 135

JULIO CORTAZAR.
COMRADE IN PRISON AND IN FREEDOM. 145

NOTES 154

CREATIVITY IN THE REVOLUTION: THE LITERARY BORGE

By Way of an Introduction.

Like many Nicaraguans, Tomás Borge is a poet.

He is also the "old man" of Nicaragua's Sandinista revolution and one of the most polemical figures in contemporary Central America. Portrayed in the United States and elsewhere as a political hard-liner and "Marxist ideologue", he stands at the center of the widening conflict between the guardians of empire and the challengers of imperial dominion.

In marked contrast to the cultural poverty of political leadership in Washington and the outlying redoubts of U.S. hegemony, Borge, like many of his colleagues in Nicaragua's revolutionary government, is an exceptionally literate man. Indeed, his strong poetic bent and proclivity to literary pursuits, combined with a profound sense of human solidarity rooted in the traditions of Christianity, reflect a decisive feature of the Nicaraguan experience: a people's determined quest for their own humanity endows them with a wisdom and strength far beyond their numbers.

In this sense Borge's diminutive physical stature perhaps symbolizes the geographic and numerical smallness of Nicaragua next to the United States, a continental collossus that seeks to remake all Central America in its own image. Likewise, his uncompromising patriotism and political resolve reflect the dignity and resourcefulness of a besieged people determined to surmount the harsh legacy of imperial bondage and material underdevelopment.

In the lexicon of the developed world, a U.S. poet once observed, the term *underdevelopment* implies "that the people are underdeveloped, that they have an underdeveloped morality or an underdeveloped sense of culture or an underdeveloped understanding of the world."[1] This is certainly true of North American attitudes toward

Nicaragua, which now suffers the consequences of U.S. "underdevelopment" and the arrogance it feeds — that same arrogance that denies Tomás Borge an entry visa to the United States lest his views and persona become known to the U.S. public.

For eight years the Reagan Administration in fact made a concerted effort to discredit Borge and to tarnish him personally. The demonization of prominent historical actors by their adversaries, of course, is a common, if transparent, practice that dates from the origins of organized society. By dehumanizing one's opponents, it becomes possible to destroy them without doing undue injury to established ethical constraints.

Thus efforts to defame Tomás Borge and to delegitimize the Sandinista revolution in the public's eye have focused precisely on the revolution's defining morality, on its humanitarian priorities. Repeated attempts have been made, for example, to link Borge to international narcotics trafficking and in general to associate him with behavior that would negate the very bases of the revolution. The cynicism of these efforts and the total divorce of the allegations from reality warrant unmitigated reproach.[2] The present volume, for its part, seeks to provide insight into the mind and personality of Tomás Borge for readers in the United States, that they might better appreciate the central issues posed by the Sandinista revolution and the real nature of their own country's relentless assault on their Nicaraguan neighbors.[3]

* * * * *

If St. Francis of Assisi was the decisive influence in Tomás Borge's moral development,[4] Augusto César Sandino defined his sense of patriotism. Borge was four years old when Sandino was betrayed and assassinated by Anastasio Somoza García, founder of the despised Somoza dynasty and a creature of U.S. intervention.[5] He was seven when Somoza agents murdered Sandino's most trusted comrade in arms, General Pedro Altamirano.

As a young man Borge read everything he could find about Sandino and his struggle against U.S. domination, continuing to study and meditate on the life and thought of Nicaragua's national hero down to the present. "When Sandino, with a handful of men, rebelled against the North American intervention," Borge asserts, "he placed Nicaragua's definitive stamp on its history. By that act Sandino traced Nicaragua's future course, the one it now follows, a course marked by Sandino's struggle and sacrifice."[6]

Borge would seem to have retrieved Sandino's mantle, emulating the fallen "General of Free Men" in his own life. He was born and raised in the northern mountain town of Matagalpa, where he felt Sandino's presence from earliest childhood. He met Sandino's father, Don Gregorio, at the house of an uncle, Sofonías Salvatierra, and would listen to the elder Sandino recount the historic deeds of his renowned son.

Borge's father, Tomás Alberto, had known Sandino personally and delighted in showing photographs in which he and Sandino could be seen embracing. It was even said that there was a family tie to Sandino, although Borge has been unable to corroborate a blood relationship. Be that as it may, he affirms, like many Nicaraguans, "I feel that through my veins flow the dreams and blood of Sandino."[7]

Carlos Fonseca Amador, the moving force behind and first leader of the Sandinista National Liberation Front (FSLN), also grew up in Matagalpa. He and Borge were schoolmates and already as boys manifested their first overt opposition to the Somoza dictatorship. It was Fonseca who later, as a fellow student at the University of León, impressed on Borge the political and historical transcendency of Sandino.[8]

Carlos Fonseca, Borge recounts in the allegorical manner for which he is known, "was a kind of actuator of Sandino's thought. It was like the cry of Christ when he said to Lazarus: 'Arise and walk!' Sandino had been buried and had pretended to be dead. And Somoza, who murdered him, believed he had killed him for all time. Then along came Carlos Fonseca and he said to Sandino: 'Arise and walk!' And Sandino arose and began to walk. And he hasn't stopped since. That, I feel, is the great historical merit of Carlos Fonseca."[9]

History, biblical parable, and poetry are the guiding vehicles by which Borge interprets and moves through the world. From a disciplined reading of the past he searches out the historical roots of his own people and of contemporary reality. At the same time, he grounds his moral self on the traditions of Christian humanism, while constantly probing the subjective side of human behavior in the pages of literature and his own creative writing.

"At eleven o'clock one night," he recalls, "while my mother thought I was singeing my eyelashes on the problems of 'reasoned arithmetic' and the subtleties of verbal moods, Winnetou died against a backdrop of stupefied twilight. Winnetou, fraternal friend of Old Shatterhand, hunter of buffalo and falsehoods, enemy of fear, archetypal Indian of the North American West, invulnerable to pain and impatience, was the man we wished to be."

Winnetou had died and lay buried "beneath grass trampled by wild horses and in the pages of an account that surely is not a novel," Borge writes, for one could understand "that in real life so beloved a hero might die, while it would be unpardonable for Karl May to make us suffer so much due to a whim of his imagination." Winnetou's virtues, "his loyalty, rectitude, acceptance of risk, inability to lie and readiness to defend the humble," he insists, "were not interred with his beautiful, bronzed, muscular body."[10] Winnetou became Borge's life model. "Since I couldn't live in the Old West of the U.S.," he relates, "I tried to apply these values to the injustices and hardships my own people faced here in Nicaragua."[11]

This melding of moral principle, objective analysis and literary imagination is the salient characteristic of Borge's personal conduct and approach to the world around him. Julio Cortázar has described it as "that difficult alliance of poetic sensitivity with the hard responsibility of leading a people toward their authentic destiny, that iron will, which, extending its hand, squeezes without hurting."[12] And Borge's poetic sensitivity is apparent throughout. It is what enabled him to survive the ordeal of imprisonment and the arduous struggle against the Somoza tyranny.

It is even reflected suggestively in his *nom de guerre,* Brother Wolf, which was taken from Rubén Darío's allegoric poem, "Los motivos del lobo" (Motives of the Wolf), about St. Francis and the wolf, wherein the wolf is unable to heed St. Francis' plea to live in harmony with human beings because he cannot abide their envy, malice, ire, hatred, lust, infamy and lies.[13] During Borge's final period of imprisonment prior to the triumph of the Sandinista revolution in July 1979, comrade in arms Henry Ruiz addressed a letter to Brother Wolf in which he wrote: "Today you no longer need your elevator shoes, for you have grown, you are soaring; your detractors must bite their tongues, because determination is more than just a word; it is palpable deeds in the hands and face of the enemy. Determination means steadfastness, moral strength and proven ideas. Therein lie the roots of the new man."[14]

* * * * *

The story of Tomás Borge's imprisonment and torment at the hands of Somoza jailers is by now well known. He was captured by National Guardsmen in February 1976, hooded, manacled, and tortured for the next nine months. He was tried by a military tribunal, sentenced to 180 years in prison, and kept in solitary confinement until his dramatic release in August 1978, when an FSLN commando unit seized the National Palace in Managua and forced the dictator to free over fifty Sandinista prisoners.

Allowed limited reading material and periodic visits by his companion, Josefina, Borge coped with his confinement during that final year and a half by writing, composing poetry and reading. His preferred books were the *Bible* and the works of Argentine literary giant Julio Cortázar, with whom he subsequently developed a close friendship. As he relates in his own words below, his prison poems were therapy, an effort to recover his humanity and the ability to express himself following the long months of brutalization to which he had been subjected.

These and other creative writings by Borge provide important insight into the character and personality of a key architect of Nicaragua's revolutionary society. They give the lie to the endless calumnies directed against Borge and the Sandinista revolution from the United States. The present selection of writings seeks to provide the English-speaking reader with a sense of the literary Borge, which is also the ethical and the political Borge.

* * * * *

The poetry and prose that follow span over thirty years of Borge's life, ranging from an early short story about his university days ("Story Number Two") to a poetic statement of revolutionary purpose completed in late 1987 ("Repression"). This selection offers examples of both creative and critical writing, which taken together provide insight into the evolution of Borge's literary sensibilities and the inextricable relationship of those sensibilities to the larger socio-historical milieu that defines Borge as a writer, poet and political actor. These materials are given added dimension by Borge's own words about himself, offered in conversation with the editors of this volume.

The two sections of poetry, in turn, reflect different moments in Borge's life and thus his own evolution as a poet. His "clandestine poems," introduced here by acclaimed fellow poet Carlos Martínez Rivas and grouped as they originally appeared in 1975 under the pseudonym Jairó Reyes Becerra, are examples of the spontaneity and automatism of his poetic creativity in the guerrilla underground, where he penned verse on easily lost scraps of paper for his friends. Of particular interest here is Borge's commitment to the surrealist image — as noted by Martínez Rivas — in striking contrast to the "exteriorist" mode which has characterized Nicaraguan poetry since the 1950s.[15]

With the exception of "The Awaited Ceremony" (1973), composed while in exile, the second section of verse comprises Borge's "prison poems" and several examples of recent poetry. Among the latter, his lengthy poem, "Repression", exemplifies the creative dilemma of the recognized poet to which Martínez Rivas alludes in his introductory observations (p. 39). This is no longer the unencumbered, anonymous poetry of the clandestine revolutionary, rather the deliberately crafted verse of a public personage. Initially titled "Ordeno" (I Order) and first published under that title while the present volume was in preparation,[16] Borge subsequently revised and retitled this poem in the version that appears below. "I Am Not", "Yours, Mine", "There It Was", "Che" and "The Gentle Condition", in turn, are examples of Borge's latest poetic endeavors. They reflect some of the earlier spontaneity of his clandestine period, as well as the irrepressible need of the poet/revolutionary to express the poetic essences of political conflict. While these poems are of unequal literary merit, in their very unevenness they bear witness to the committed poet struggling mightily against the deadening restraints of a prosaic world.

The prose pieces included here complement Borge's poetry, shedding additional light on the spiritual and creative resources of a man deeply committed to the humanization of contemporary society. They further reveal the depth and breadth of his literary vocation. His personal account of incarceration during the dictatorship ("From the Model Prison") is at once an historical and literary document, while his moving "Letter to Ana Josefina" is itself a poetic testament. "Macho Malo," an allegory for Nicaraguan children, reflects his consummate ability to combine literary imagination with moral parable and political purpose. Likewise, his multi-leveled remarks about Nicaraguan poet laureate José Coronel Urtecho contribute to a fuller understanding of Nicaragua's cultural, as well as political history. And finally, Borge's stunning essay on Julio Cortázar exhibits the full vitality of his poetic and literary self, of his humanity, integrity and creative sensitivity.

Like many Nicaraguans, he is a poet.

* * * * *

As with any work of translation, the present volume is itself a creative endeavor. It is by definition interpretive and thus the product of an inevitable subjectivity. That is not to say, however, that it lacks objective criteria either in content or translation. This has been a collaborative undertaking to which the editors bring extensive experience as translators, writers, and individuals personally familiar with Nicaragua. The translations themselves are the result of consensus achieved through a disciplined, at times exhausting, consideration of all disputable points. They are, we feel, faithful reflections of the Spanish originals.

Again, the primary purpose of this volume is to provide the English-speaking reader with a sense of Tomás Borge as a writer and a poet, that is, of the literary Borge. It is not in the strictest sense a scholarly work, rather a modest anthology of original writings in translation. Accordingly, we have limited annotations to those points requiring clarification for the general reader. Critical analyses and references remain for future studies.

Milwaukee/Bowling Green
December 1988

HAVE YOU SEEN A RED CURTAIN
IN MY WEARY CHAMBER?

Tomás Borge reciting one of his poems, February 1986.

WE'RE A COUNTRY OF OPEN WINDOWS

A Conversation with Tomás Borge Martínez
(April 1987)

When did you start writing poetry?

I've always written poetry. What happened was that all the poetry I've written has been lost — in the underground, during the war, in exile. All that's left is what I have here and some that I wrote while I was in Colombia.

When was that?

That was about 1970 — seventy, seventy-one.

And how did poetry come into your life?

The first poetry I read was Darío's, when I was very young. At my father's urging I read practically everything Darío had written. I also read a lot of mythology when I was young, that, too, at my father's suggestion. I think that must have influenced my early interest in writing poetry.

It seems you were always a studious person. What attracted you to literature and the arts?

My father's influence was decisive in arousing my interest in reading. My father possessed a vast library, one of the most complete of his day. He also bought and sold books.

Do you recall the first poem you ever wrote?

I believe the first poem I ever wrote was called "The Mountain". It was a really nice poem. I was eleven when I wrote it. It talked about the jungle, about the mountains, about the dense foliage. Yes, I remember it well.

How is it that your poetry has been lost?

I've lost almost all the poetry I've ever written. Relatively little has survived inasmuch as I wrote all my poems while I was underground, during the war, or while I was in exile. I would write them on scraps of paper that were easily lost and now it's impossible to recover them. So, except for the poetry I wrote in Colombia, some of which has been saved, most of the poems I wrote in Cuba, here in Nicaragua and in other countries has been lost. And it's probably just as well!

You seem to have a tendency to belittle your poetry. Indeed, until very recently you were disinclined to publish any of the poems you have managed to preserve.

Some of my poems were published under a pseudonym in *La Prensa Literaria* while I was underground. This was done at the initiative of our compañera, Rosario Murillo. I have felt ever since that poetry is not really something you do for publication. With good reason it has been said that poetry is an internal form of expression. I think that's true not only from a strictly literary point of view, but also in the sense that poetry entails a certain self-centered appropriation of verbal expression that at times proves unintelligible to others.

Nonetheless, you now seem interested in publishing your poems.

I myself am not interested. But friends have asked me repeatedly to publish some of what I have written. Eduardo Galeano, a close friend of mine, has asked me to publish. You folks, who also are my friends, have asked me. And various Nicaraguan poets, among them Carlos Martínez Rivas, have asked me. I myself have always feared that power and political fame might draw more attention to my poetry than it really merits.

Briefly, what were the circumstances in which you wrote your prison poems?

When I began writing those poems I had just spent several long months in solitary confinement, manacled and with a hood covering my eyes the whole time. It was an effort to recover my ability to express myself. I was not allowed to write while I was in prison, so I had to do it surreptitiously. With the help of my companion, Josefina, I managed to smuggle them out. The way I did it was to remove the tobacco from cigarettes, carefully wrap the poems in the cigarette paper and then replace the tobacco so that they looked like ordinary cigarettes.

While you were in prison you also wrote a very moving letter to your little daughter, Ana Josefina, who at the time was celebrating her second birthday. Can you tell us a little bit about that letter?

When my daughter was born, I went to the hospital to see her, which constituted a grave violation of security that almost cost me my life because the Guard was alerted and I had to slip through their lines when they were already encircling the hospital. In any event, love and the illusion of seeing my infant daughter, Ana Josefina, moved me two years later, while in prison, to write that letter expressing my tenderness for her and the emotion I felt just knowing that she existed. Moreover, when I wrote that letter I didn't know if I would ever see her again. So, it was also a kind of final testament.

On a more abstract level, what do you see as the proper relationship between artistic expression and the larger needs of the revolutionary process? Is there not perhaps a conflict between the individual's need to express personal sentiments and the imperatives of the Revolution?

The Revolution is really an everyday routine, the daily tasks of preparing memoranda, instructions and institutional communications — technical, mechanical, invariable tasks. I think the inevitable bureaucracy hinders the gestation of poetry, which at times nonetheless cannot be ignored, just as a pregnancy requires a birth. I find it difficult to write poetry while immersed in paper work and daily operations.

But, in more general terms, there are those who express concerns that the Revolution exerts pressure on artists with regard to both the form and the content of their works. What is the relationship between artistic creativity as such and the political exigencies of the revolutionary process? What are the artist's obligations vis-à-vis the Revolution?

I think the artist's primary obligation is to produce art. In that sense, the artist should not be obliged to turn out art on assignment, which almost always produces bad results. It produces painting or poetry that's gray, pale, deficient.

Sometimes, however, the revolutionary process itself, its ongoing programs, the people's heroism, give rise to works of art, as has happened with great singers and composers like Carlos Mejía, or with a whole array of artists throughout Nicaraguan history, or occasionally with sculpture, as in the case of Ernesto Cardenal, who not only is a great poet but an excellent sculptor as well. There is even a sculpture by Ernesto Cardenal in the new Olaf Palme Convention Center.

In all that's been written and said about the culture and cultural transformation of Nicaragua, there is almost no reference to children or young people. Why is that?

For reasons that are somewhat difficult to explain, there is very little children's poetry or literature in Nicaragua. I say difficult to explain because the Revolution has attached particular importance to children. They've been called the Revolution's pampered ones. Lately, however, I think we are seeing the beginnings of a children's literature that has yet to surface but is already in existence.

The Atlantic Coast has occupied its own peculiar place in the history of Nicaragua. How does coastal culture relate to creativity and cultural expression within the framework of the Revolution and its quest for a new national identity?

In the past it was nothing more than a vague allusion of commercialized folklore for tourists, an anecdote of "erotic" music and dances with occasional English lyrics for export.

Today things are different. The national liberation of Nicaragua, of which coastal autonomy is a necessary condition, has generated an explosion of creativity and is moving people to interpret a multitude of life experiences in dance, music, theater, painting and other art forms. How people think cannot remain unaffected by the transformation of Nicaraguan society, by the teaching of literacy skills in the country's indigenous tongues, by the introduction of radio and television into the Atlantic Coast, by the publication of our first bilingual texts.

Then, too, there has been a generalized expansion of contacts with the Pacific Coast and its particular cultural expressions. This can only give rise to a wider range of cultural expressions throughout the country. They will each preserve their own unique features, of course, and that's as it should be, but the ultimate expression of Nicaraguan society, on the cultural as well as other levels, lies in a multiplicity of expressions.

You yourself have become deeply involved in the affairs of the Atlantic Coast. How did this come about, or have you always had ties to the Coast? How does the Atlantic Coast make itself felt in your own sense of identity as a Nicaraguan? Is it reflected at all in your poetry or other writings?

I remember that as a young man I once remarked to a close relative that there was Indian blood in my veins. We were blood relatives. And he replied, "In yours, perhaps, but not in mine..."

My involvement with the Atlantic Coast is an inevitable part of my identification with the Nicaraguan people. From Sandino's day to the present the communities of our Atlantic slope have played a role in the struggle for our liberation. How could one not be involved with them? Moreover, one's sense of identity as a Nicaraguan is heightened and refined to the degree that we have all come to comprehend the cultural, social and moral richness contained in a multi-ethnic, multi-lingual and multi-cultural nation.

My own responsibilities as president of the National Commission on the Autonomy of the Atlantic Coast have made me much more aware of the sensibilities of the coastal population and I have understood the legitimate historic nature of their demands, as well as come to appreciate the fullness and richness of the Miskito language, which I have felt obliged to study.

I believe that all Nicaraguans are being enriched by this experience, which I expect will be reflected in the release of new creative energies in everyone. In my own case, it has thus far only produced some reflections in a few speeches and in an article published as a supplement in *Barricada* in late November 1986. I would not dismiss the possibility, however, that sometime in the future it might be the source of a literary effort. But what matters in all this is that we come to give meaning to our dreams of a national identity. Once we achieve this, I have not the slightest doubt that this essential achievement will serve as an inspiration for all manner of creativity.

One of the major problems faced by a country like Nicaragua is what has been called "cultural imperialism". How, in your view, can this problem be resolved? Is it possible for a country like Nicaragua to escape foreign cultural domination?

I think one must be able to distinguish between the influence of North American culture, even contemporary U.S. culture, which cannot be rejected out of hand, and the influence of an alienated culture designed by the hierarchs of expansion and domination to serve the ends of oppression and dependency.

In the United States there are extraordinary cultural reserves and an enormous cultural heritage in both music and literature. I am referring not only to classic U.S. literature, to their great novelists of world renown, nor to justly acclaimed American jazz and North American music in general, rather to art forms of the present moment, to everyday expressions that must be perceived, understood and cherished.

Overall, I think there is a creative pluralism in the United States that makes it possible to create art, not just the canned, alienated, brutal "art" the North Americans sometimes send us for our people's consumption. There is, perhaps, in the United States a certain poverty of institutionalized art. I, at least, am not familiar with any magazines or specialized publications that feature the enormous cultural potential of the American people. We are, on the other hand, quite familiar with publications like the *Reader's Digest,* which are really packaged poison, publications whose purpose is to perturb, to distract and to confuse the peoples of the world ideologically and politically.

How are you to control that within a revolution committed to cultural pluralism?

In Nicaragua we receive U.S. films and television programs. Not many North American magazines circulate here, not even the *Reader's Digest.* But I think that's more a matter of scarce hard currency than any deliberate policy on our part. Fortunately, it just isn't possible for those U.S. publications that would poison our people to enter the country, although we do receive and show — albeit to a lesser extent than in other countries — U.S. films and television programs. That's because there is no substitute. I don't mean to speak against North American cinema, which has produced great works of art, but it is unfortunate that U.S. films have not yet been replaced by our own revolutionary cinema, which thus far lacks resources and imagination — although there do seem to be some recent advances in Cuba and even in the Soviet Union, where in the early stages of the Bolshevik Revolution film achieved incalculable heights.

Yet for the Sandinista Revolution the problem remains the same: in order to promote new values it is necessary to deal with the reality of foreign cultural influence.

We have everything here. We're a country of open windows that allow in both foul odors and the sweetest of fragrances. Here the innovative, our own concrete production, induces us to be optimistic in the struggle against cultural forms that might deteriorate the revolutionary process.

STORY NUMBER TWO[1]

"I hate you! I hate you!" Rodolfo turned pale.

"I hate you, damn it!"

To me these last words penetrated like the whistle of a bootblack.

"I hate you!" Margarita repeated, her anger undiminished, like the prayer litany of an old witch.

Margarita was, however, young and beautiful.

In her eyes there shone such fury that I, the inevitable spectator, abandoned the Hemingway novel I had just started with Christian resignation, like all resignation, trivial and obvious.

My classmate Adrian — an Atlantic Coast black — opened his eyes wide like two circles drawn on a blackboard.

"I hate you!"

We all began to tire of that bitter unpublished poem. Our impatience turned objective: Adrian abandoned the book into which he had all but thrust his nose to feign concentration, while I went back to shaving my beard with the edge of the Hemingway volume.

Rodolfo got up brusquely from the chair to which he'd been nailed as though on a newly built cross. Shaking the girl by her shoulders he said: "Shut up! You make me sick!" And turning to us: "Forgive me, gentlemen, but I can't help it. This makes me sick."

The exchange burst forth like dirty water. The coarse words spilled out like rolls of barbed wire. Their soiled linen was aired like flags in the sun . . .

I had a bitter taste in my mouth and felt a strange tingling sensation in my intestines.

I closed my eyes. It was, after all, a quarrel between newlyweds.

In a penultimate gesture Rodolfo spat, then, over his sweaty undershirt, he pulled on a well ironed shirt as clean as a hospital sheet. Finally, he went out into the street. That night he'd return drunk and stinking of brothels.

Meanwhile, Margarita seemed to calm down. She continued to grumble, however, biting her upper lip with her small, perfect teeth, parodying the latest baseball hero. Margarita's imitation wasn't bad, her lower lip hanging smooth, rosy and sensuous.

Adrian shrugged his shoulders.

"My dear doctor," he said to me, *"definitivamente ésta es una pensión de mierda.* Shame on you. *Muy interesante la novela de Jack London.* Earful. *Pero definitivamente hoy cambio mi programa. Voy a clase."*[2]

Adrian annoyed me sometimes with his pedantic bilingualism. He knew English, or at least I thought he did. Moreover, he was charming, as ingenious as a courtesan, dignified like most blacks, a good dancer, and a little melodramatic. Tossing his gray frock coat over his lithe shoulders, he walked out, his engaging smile enticing patrons' looks as he went.

"So long."

I definitely wasn't going to class. It was easier to continue savoring my idle neighbor's rose colored dress while lying on my back reading Hemingway's bearded book. It was, after all, a deserved vacation, for I had just passed a class I had previously flunked.

I was trying to recall the page which, at the moment of the inopportune "I hate you's", I had attempted to memorize, when a shadow slipped to my side.

"Forgive my disturbing you, doctor." Margarita's voice had changed to a tone between piquant and servile.

"I repeat to you once again," I replied with a frown, "I'm not a doctor. I will be in a few years. If you must give me a title, call me *bachiller.*[3] Or simply call me Mario."

The girl dragged a chair over to where I was stretched out on a kind of camp cot.

"What's your opinion of all this?"

"What's 'all this'?"

"You know what I mean, Don Mario."

"Do you mean, what do I think of your husband?"

"And of me."

I began to think this wasn't a conversation, rather a pretext. Feigning distraction, Margarita adjusted one of her garters.

"Well, you're pretty . . ." I said clumsily.

"Do you like me?" The girl didn't blush, but she feigned embarassment.

"Well . . ."

"You do like me...What do you know! And my husband likes white cunt! The problem is I demand respect."

The young woman seemed to turn pensive. Then, yawning, she drew her chair closer to my head.

"Today he's going to come back drunk," she mused.

"Who?"

"Who? My husband, that's who! He's going to come back drunk, I tell you, breaking chairs and wanting to hit me. But . . you're going to defend me, aren't you?"

"Of course," I said, prudently not giving much emphasis to my reply.

"Thanks. Thanks a lot!"

The girl drew so close that I could smell the scent of her hair. It was an asphyxiating and intoxicating scent. As intoxicating as a glass of booze after a night of partying.

Without looking at her I knew her eyes were fixed on my clenched fists. Twenty-four hours before I had read the final chapter of Leo Tolstoy's novel, *Resurrection.* After reading that novel one can only be chaste. Superficially chaste, if you wish; or well-intentioned, at any rate.

I pulled abruptly away.

"Well, Margarita, I'm also changing my plans. I'm going to class."

She lowered her eyes in silence, abashed. Genuinely ashamed. So ashamed that even her scalp turned red. I, too, was ashamed of her shame and in spite of everything my lungs filled with a vague sense of frustration.

I would make only the end of the class. That, however, was no obstacle to my pride, for I was a hero! Without a doubt, I was a hero! Like Tolstoy's protagonist, repentant after dishonoring a girl who loved him, I was moved almost to tears by my own heroism.

I began to walk slowly, head held high as befits an extraordinary man. The leather heels of my shoes resounded like a drum on the pavement. Only the bugle was missing. But I didn't notice.

Turning my head from left to right, looking with disdain on poor, weak, sinning humanity, I opened and closed my eyes aloofly.

A toothless, wrinkled old woman stood watching me, doubtless admiring the dignified bearing of this strong, self-sacrificing man.

How pedantic.

As if on command, I did an about-face. An about-face in the style of a newly graduated cadet.

The old woman continued watching me with hatred. Bile poured from her eyes like blood from a fresh wound. The liver is impertinent. How pedantic and inane. The old woman's voice sounded like an order from a sargeant with 25 years' service.

Slowly, I made another about-face, this one with the clumsiness of a schoolboy. All my arrogance crumbled like a poorly constructed edifice. I arrived at the University. My companions' happy laughter and ringing voices comforted me. That building was a temple, the laughter and voices an unconscious prayer of human brotherhood. I timidly approached the classroom. The professor, fat-cheeked, severe and vain, raised his glasses like a pilot after a flight.

"Mario Arrieta, you're a vagrant!"

* * * * *

The days and months passed with a certain charming monotony: parties; insipid, antipedagogical reading assignments; bombastic speeches by serious, inevitably wise men; pedantic lectures by visiting foreigners, always elegant and erudite; patriotic meetings; girls with fleshy or skinny legs, as exhibitionist as the professors; obscene jokes; novels by Howard Fast, Steinbeck, Manolo Cuadra, Flaubert, Gallegos, and even Victor Hugo. All of this repeated again and again like the disorderly shuffling of a card deck.

Back at the rooming house everything was going well.

Margarita was pregnant.

It was curious how she came and went about her domestic chores, her recriminatory impulses and adulterous inclinations having subsided. At times, only at times, the fetus seems to be an enormous tranquilizer.

Rodolfo's serene.

At least he can be happy nine months of the year. Others are wretched the whole 365 days, he said to Adrian one day. "*Animo pues,* my dear guy."[4]

The birth arrived as inevitably do all things in this life. A simple birth, without metaphysics or complications: a cheap doctor, some hot towels and a million units of penicillin.

Adrian won the bet. It was a boy. From that day on the little critter, rosy as a maiden's blush, gave out his impertinent cries at precisely the pertinent times.

We counted the days as impatiently as a young boy says the rosary when he wants to go to the movies to see a western. Everything was calm. The long months passed like the seasons of the year. Complete calmness.

One afternoon Adrian and I were heading for class when we saw Margarita and Rodolfo. Both were smiling in the midst of an animated conversation. Nothing but smiles. We wouldn't have believed it. But they were talking. An animated, mutually shared conversation is the best symptom of conjugal harmony.

There was a pure, new light in Margarita's eyes.

Between husband and wife the child, too, was conversing with his smile, extending his arms to entwine his little fingers in his parents' hands. That magnificent trinity — archetype of the sacred family — seemed a Monument.

The couple exchanged a theatrical kiss to show us that they loved each other.

Adrian offered the tablets of his mouth to passersby.

"*Definitivamente,*[5] my friend . . ."

I began to whistle a popular *bolero*. I always do that when I'm happy.

"Roman Law" wasn't quite so important that day.

21 November 1955

Borge discussing a new poem with Francisco de Asís, Nicaraguan poet.

CLANDESTINE POEMS AND PROSE

CLANDESTINE POEMS AND PROSE

Critical Comments by Carlos Martínez Rivas.[1]

When I read some of Tomás Borge's poems and listened to a recorded interview with him, I realized that within the larger body of Nicaraguan poetry of his generation, his poetry was unusual, and that in its own way the interview actually complemented those poems, even though in it Borge was loath to talk about his literary "inclinations" and limited his responses on the subject to the briefest of replies.

He stated that he writes his poems in less than ten minutes, that he never rereads or edits them, and that he writes his poems with no thought to preserving them, always giving them away to friends. Along with this statement, however, Borge provided a lengthy and varied list of works he has read, making special mention of the Latin American "boom" novelists, among whom his favorites are Julio Cortázar and Garbriel García Márquez. He made a number of observations about both these authors, noting their historical contemporaneity as well as their fundamental differences of temperament. Thus the fact that he is at once a voracious and discerning reader contradicted Borge's impatient, even contemptuous attitude toward his own literary endeavors. That attitude is further contradicted by his *memoire* or biographical sketch of Carlos Fonseca Amador, *Carlos, The Dawn Is No Longer Beyond Our Reach.*[2]

This enticing little volume about Carlos Fonseca is dominated by a concise, poetic style devoid of metaphorical excesses and epigrammatic affectation — *Doña Bárbara* and *Don Segundo Sombra* come immediately to mind[3] — yet filled with direct, unadorned narration imbued now and then with the added force of a syntactical turn or adjectival formulation that are not only the indisputable, but the irrepressible creations of the poet — the poet of language, whose adjectives do not sound forced, rather opposed and always startling. There is tenderness in his description of individuals, whom he depicts with comradely respect, avoiding the vice of contrived deformation, so prevalent since the appearance and success of *One Hundred Years of Solitude*.[4]

Teresita's freckles are "important." Carlos Fonseca's eyes are "brusque, myopic and blue," his gestures "expansive." This last adjective imparts length to his fraternal arms. "Pegged" pants implies long legs and slender ankles, and thus a full-bodied man. "Sandino is not an event out of the past, not an annual disturbance, rather a kind of path." Nicaragua is "a country that exports beautiful, honed words." (How José Coronel must have enjoyed reading this!) On page 62, chapter XX, there is a moving poem about an eleven-year-old girl who dies. It's right out of Chekhov: the same economy of resources, yet less distant, more committed.

Now that these poems are being reprinted in a new intellectual atmosphere, it is worth making a few critical observations on their style and content so as to situate them in the context of Nicaraguan poetry of the early 1970s. Not only are poetry books of the highest quality being produced in those years (in such quantity that memory recoils in fear of omitting some important title), but the appearance as well of new young poets in magazines and newspapers only confirms what Don Salomón de la Selva once said: "In Nicaragua (poetic) talent is epidemic!"[5]

Yet this poetic talent has been limited to three tendencies: protest poetry, which turns its eyes to the sociocultural and political setting, intellectual or intellectualist poetry, and exteriorist poetry. With the exception of *Labyrinth of Swords* (1974), an impenetrable, Minotauric example of verbal splendor, surrealism does not appear in Nicaragua in the 1940s when José Coronel Urtecho — inspired by the left and the braided verbiage of the times — writes the poems of his osseous period, those explorations of the slimy, subliminal self, of which "Portrait of Thy Neighbor's Wife" is his supreme achievement.[6]

It simply doesn't happen that way. Surrealism "appears" in Nicaragua without anyone realizing it. These poems by Borge were first published in *La Prensa Literaria* on 23 August 1975. Yet the surrealism of these poems, while orthodox, does not belong to any of the distinctive modalities characteristic of the poems of José Coronel's osseous period or of Francisco Valle's *Labyrinth of Swords.*[7]

An original and typically surrealist element in Borge's poems is humor, the humor of love distorted by deceit, with its moments of light emanating from the creationist milieu of the period.[8] From Joaquín Pasos: "a new automobile enamored of a flower".[9] Or from Carlos Oquendo de Amat: "somebody's mother's telephone"/ "your mouth spouts ascendant gestures"/ "cyclists peddle cheap images." The poetry of this Peruvian poet, whom we cite in passing, was all produced before age 23. By the time he wrote it, the author, who was a member of the Communist Party, had already suffered prison in his country. He would do so again in Panama, on his way to Europe. He died in Madrid at age 30.

As for the surrealist humor of these poems, it is helpful to mention Ramón Gómez de la Serna[10] so as to point out one of their most noteworthy virtues, which is also a virtue of the great RAMON, who is its inventor: associative dissociation — the faculty, or more precisely, the unimpaired freedom to give flow to the most bizarre, yet obvious and graspable associations. A few examples: "a river bearing its inevitable anniversary gesture"/ "they came up, sat dawn and returned to their crusty lair"/ "earthly fire is a lion painted on a joyful mural." These are verses that bring you up short, that do not let you pass them by without returning. They are verses that give startling pause, that strike you benignly in the back of the head. One is obliged to look at things and, subconsciously, to see the correlation between them, to give them new meaning, to consider unique aspects and outcomes.

From the time of Bergson and Freud, humor appears as a metamorphosis of the spirit of defiance. It is the mask of desperation in the individualist, of revolution in the socially committed man. That is why humor as an expression of rebelliousness is a moral attitude. Humor goes straight to the prohibited zone — to insurrection. It should not surprise us, then, that the author of these poems is an insurgent, a guerrilla, a Sandinista combatant, even though his poetry belongs to what is considered an élitist, petty bourgeois literary movement.

One clarification: an error that is frequently elevated to the level of dogma is that the characteristic feature of surrealism is the dreamworld. That may be so in painting (Dalí, Tanguy, Magritte), which perhaps explains the confusion. But in literature, in poetry, its fundamental characteristic is automatic writing. This is done by the person who intentionally or involuntarily erases the rational structure of his thought or who writes in a state of trance, what in surrealist lexicon is called the "second state": a sure medium for promoting the flight of the psychic faculties and particularly artistic talent, focusing one's awareness on the task at hand and thereby freeing him from inhibiting factors that restrain and distract him, at times to the point of totally impeding the use of his latent gifts.

Automatic writing permits the individual to glimpse a new world and to balance the elements of this new world with those of the "normal" external world. Reduced to a common plane, both worlds are intermixed and become confused in one another to form a poetic whole. In this sense, authentic surrealist poems, those produced in a trance of automatic writing (Mariana Sansón Argüello?)[11], can also be characterized by their harmony of content and form, the Kantian criterion of beauty, a free-flowing monologue unprejudiced in any way by the critical spirit, unhindered by the slightest reticence, as close as possible to spoken thought.

An additional clarification: enumerative poetry, even when it lacks discursive illation, is not automatic writing. There are two classic examples in modern poetry: "Lundi rue Christine" and *Il y a,* by Guillaume Apollinaire.[12] In Nicaragua we have one incredible sample, which insofar as my limited reading experience allows me to judge, has the additional merit of being one of the most moving poems in any literature: José Coronel Urtecho's "Ciudad Quesada".[13]

As for the present automatist poems, the question arises: How is it that in Nicaragua, land of innate, congenitally exteriorist poets, there appears a lone poet given naturally to automatic writing? For the poet who writes the following poems and "prose" in 1975 is indeed generically alone when he writes them. Surrounded by local currents in vogue at the time that might well have influenced him, he does not write poetry "in arms"; he does not write "social" poetry, nor "vernacular" poetry, nor "intellectualist" poetry; he does not write "exteriorist" poetry. He writes love poetry, a poetry of Bretonian *amour fou*, transmitting it by means of convulsive imagery, as Breton himself labeled it, just as it is constituted in automatic writing. Speed and impersonalism are decisive factors in automatic writing, its ideal objective. The fact, therefore, that the author of these poems "writes them in ten minutes to give away" does not invalidate the act nor does it affect the quality of the result.

Now that "Nicaragua has returned to being a Republic", these poems published in 1975 and written by "Jairó Reyes Becerra" are being republished with their author's true name: Tomás Borge Martínez. But with an admonition: in love as in poetry — which are the same thing, especially in surrealism — new freedom presupposes new rules. To cease writing or publishing under the protection of pseudonyms, heteronyms and false epigraphs means that Tomás Borge is losing one freedom to assume another, more difficult one: the freedom to speak for himself, as a poet, in his own name and with his own name.

Captain, oh Captain, thy terrible journey has begun![14]

HAY UNA MUCHACHA

"Rappelle-tois Barbara?"
Jacques Prévert

Hay una muchacha
Es una cuerda de guitarra
Un cerillo encendido
Un trago
Un río
Con su inevitable gesto de aniversario
Me recuerda todos los días
El último acuerdo que tuvo con el sol.
Sale a la calle
Se mete en alguna oficina
Escupe frases azules
Sonríe
Para ocultar sus inútiles
Y deliciosos complejos de culpa.
No se sorprende si mira a un ángel
Orinando de los ojos de un gato
Pero le brinca la risa en la piel
Cuando no ve nada
Con sus ojos de terca adolescencia.
Cuando ella ve ríos de rosas
Que corren entre las cloacas
Cantando
Se pone seria
Corre a su casa
Y me espera.

THERE'S A GIRL

"Do you remember, Barbara?"
Jacques Prévert[14]

There's a girl
She's a guitar string
A lighted match
A drink
A river
Bearing its inevitable anniversary gesture
She reminds me daily
Of her final pact with the sun.
She goes out into the street
Vanishes into some office
Spits out blue phrases
Smiles
To mask her useless
Delicious complexes of guilt.
It does not startle her to see an angel
Urinating from the eyes of a cat
But laughter leaps on her skin
When she sees nothing
With her stubbornly adolescent eyes.
When she sees rivers of roses
Rushing through the gutters
Singing
She grows solemn
Runs home
And waits for me.

VOY A MORIR BAJO LA LLUVIA

Voy a morir bajo la lluvia
con residuos de sol en la fatiga
ayer. Voy a morir ayer.
Hoy no tengo tiempo
y mañana iré a recorrer el estampido
de todos los martillos
Cuando envejezca
cuando llegue yo a viejo
dentro de cien o mil años
desde el umbral de un pájaro
oiré la risa de los niños
y la irreversible equivocación de los insectos
No tendré ojos ni dientes sin metabolismo seré tan sólo
un largo hueso satisfecho.

"Hemos de dejar esta tierra
estamos prestados unos a otros
iremos a la casa del sol."
NEZAHUALCOYOTL

I'M GOING TO DIE IN THE RAIN

I'm going to die in the rain
with fragments of sun in my fatigue
yesterday. I'm going to die yesterday.[15]
Today I have no time
and tomorrow I'll go walk among the pounding
of all the hammers.
When I grow old
when I get to be an old man
within the next hundred or thousand years
from the threshold of some bird
I'll hear the laughter of children
and the irreversible error of insects
I'll have no eyes nor teeth. Without metabolism I'll be just
one long contented bone.

> "We shall leave this earth
> we are on loan to one another
> we will go to the house of the sun."
> NEZAHUALCOYOTL

DE SAL Y AGUA

No quiero lágrimas
quiero avenidas, ráfagas, lluvias
de risas y palabras
alegría en las uñas
luz en la infatigable
reyerta de tus ojos
tal vez una contribución
de sal y agua en la ternura
un poco de rencor
obvio
de ése que sólo puede ser
hijo del amor
golpes
a lo mejor para borrar el ladrido de los perros
pero lágrimas no
sólo golpes

OF SALT AND WATER

I don't want tears
I want avenues, wind gusts, rains
of laughter and words
joy in my fingertips
light in the indefatigable
dispute of your eyes
perhaps a contribution
of salt and water in our tenderness
a bit of rancor
obviously
of the kind that can only be
the child of love
blows
perhaps to shut out the barking of dogs
but no tears
only blows

AURORA

Simplemente es cuestión de vivir
en función de cualquier momento
ése que probablemente llegará
después de mi próximo crepúsculo
aun al borde del adiós es hermoso
sentir los soles que alumbran
como pecas en tu cara
Aurora
La próxima canción nuestro trabajo
el desbordante amor por la vida
con su tu nuestro sabor a lágrimas
a comida improvisada y retazos de sueños
el feroz apetito de un nuevo amanecer
resfrío aurora arcoiris
las verdaderas nostalgias
un pantalón una camisa
una canasta de besos
frescos como tu olor a jardín
Aurora.

AURORA

It's simply a matter of living
in accord with the moment
the one that will probably arrive
after my next twilight
even on the verge of parting it is lovely
to feel the suns shining
like freckles on your face
Aurora
The next song, our labor
overflowing love of life
with its your our flavor of tears
of hasty meals and bits of dreams
the ferocious appetite of a new dawn
chill aurora rainbow
the real nostalgias
a pair of pants a shirt
a basket of kisses
fresh as your garden fragrance
Aurora.

EN CUATRO TIEMPOS

I

Vivo desde hace muchos años
buscando un teléfono que funcione
una cañería intacta
una calle sin polvo o una avenida sin lodo
a una mujer que para con
más garantía que una perra.

II

He visto a un niño desnudo
recibir cien azotes
de su madre
por haberse caído
mientras perseguía una luciérnaga
en la calle de los bombillos apagados.

III

Anduve, anduve
buscando bajo la lluvia
una palabra de aliento
alguien que me explicara si existe
la posibilidad de algún día
poder ensartar alfiles rojos
en un rayo del sol.

IV

Vivo con la certeza
de la fortaleza de los débiles
corro.

IN FOUR MOVEMENTS

I

I've lived many years now
in search of a telephone that works
of unbroken plumbing
of a dustless street or an avenue free of mud
of a woman giving birth with
more assurance than a bitch.

II

I've seen a naked child
receive a hundred lashes
from his mother
for having fallen
while chasing a firefly
through the street of darkened bulbs.

III

I wandered and wandered
seeking a word of encouragement
in the rain
someone who would explain
if the possibility exists
of one day being able to string
red chess bishops on a beam of sun.

IV

I live with the certainty
of the strength of the weak
I run.

EN FIN

Quiero liberarme de pájaros
de frases inéditas
de este amor insensato
por las hormigas
de las jaulas liberadas
de tus dulces agujeros
en fin
de todo lo que yo amo.

IN SUM

I want to free myself of birds
of unpublished phrases
of this foolish love for ants
of open cages
of your sweet openings
in sum
of everything I love.

PROSE

Besides visiting the statue of the devil, the only one in the world according to our guide, and certainly the only one with Rock Hudson's face, I spent a week in Madrid. I did what anyone else would do. A five-dollar tour to take in the city through the windows of a bus. The bull ring, me expecting sand and blood and encountering nothing but dirt. Neither banners nor bulls. Then one night a tavern, a friend, and two women. Whiskey and water or demijohns of wine. I don't remember. Little by little I drifted into a stupor and the woman was Mercedes, Yelba, Carolina. All the familiar ones, loved and unloved. Their voices, their cheeks, their bodies getTING to me. I spoke with each one and they were all the same . . . The one I didn't know and who for that very reason could be all or any one.

They talked to me at the table, on the tablecloth, in my glass. They came up, sat down and returned to their crusty lair. Some, perhaps, even overturned the tombs. In the end it would be the same one and I fell back to my musing. Gloria's hips, Carolina's breasts, Aurora's eyes.

I remained with the nameless one who cried, without knowing why I kept filling her glass. By the time I left I was carrying a bigger load than a train of tank cars, the travel-worn ones they shunt onto sidings. I reached the hotel and was caught in a cloudburst. Without warning it struck me in the eyelids and even the surprised pillow winced. I removed my eyes and hung them in the sky so as to sleep without seeing, fists clenched and history, my life story, exposed like a splayed fan.

Now when I recall that cloudburst, when the phantom of the Puerta del Sol, the Gran Vía or any other street comes back to me, I know that for me there were three things in Madrid: a hangover, a deluge, and the sadness of betraying the devil, for God has his saints, while poor Lucifer, Beelzebub, Lillith or whatever you want to call him, remains alone in his park. Everyone hurries by, some making the sign of the cross so that he shouldn't look at them or bring them misfortune.

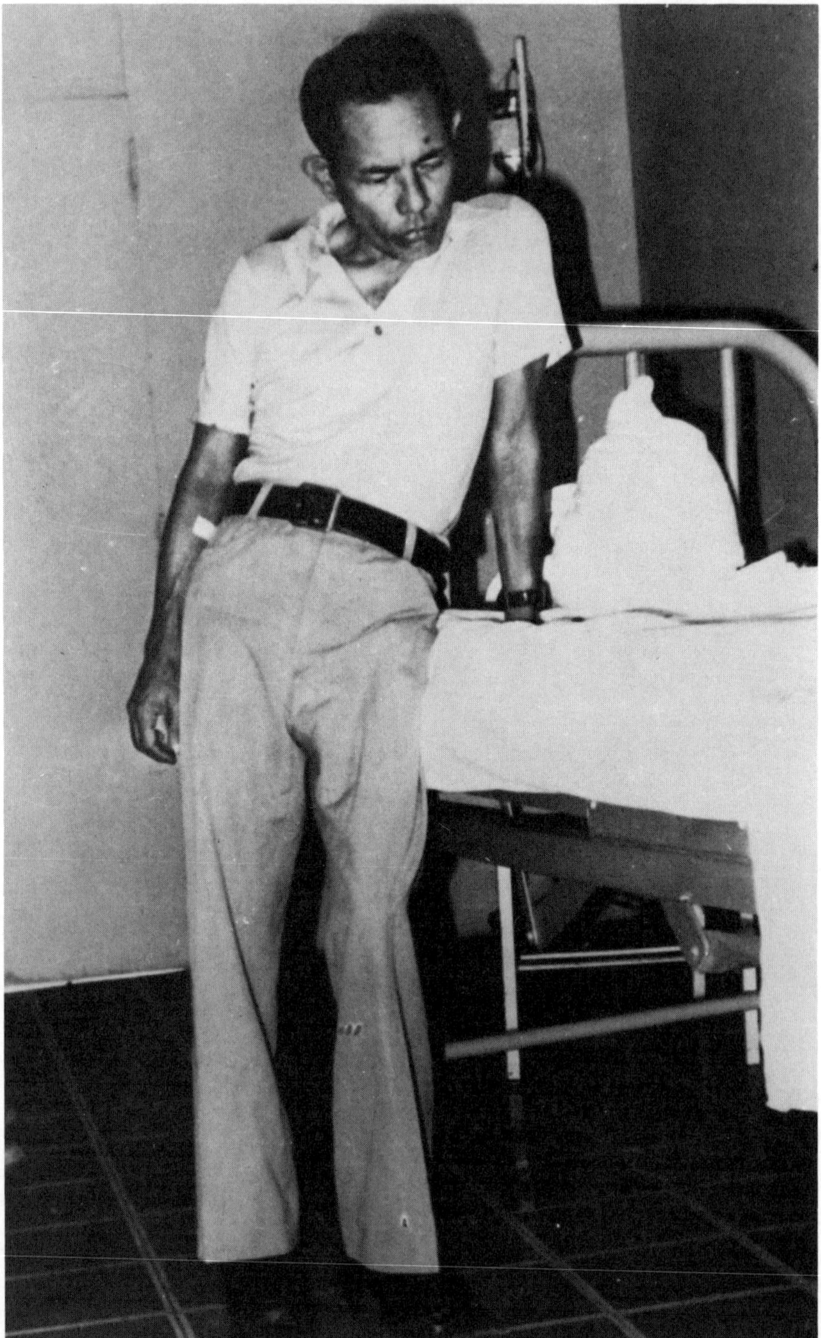

Tomás Borge debilitated by hunger strike in Tipitapa Model Prison.

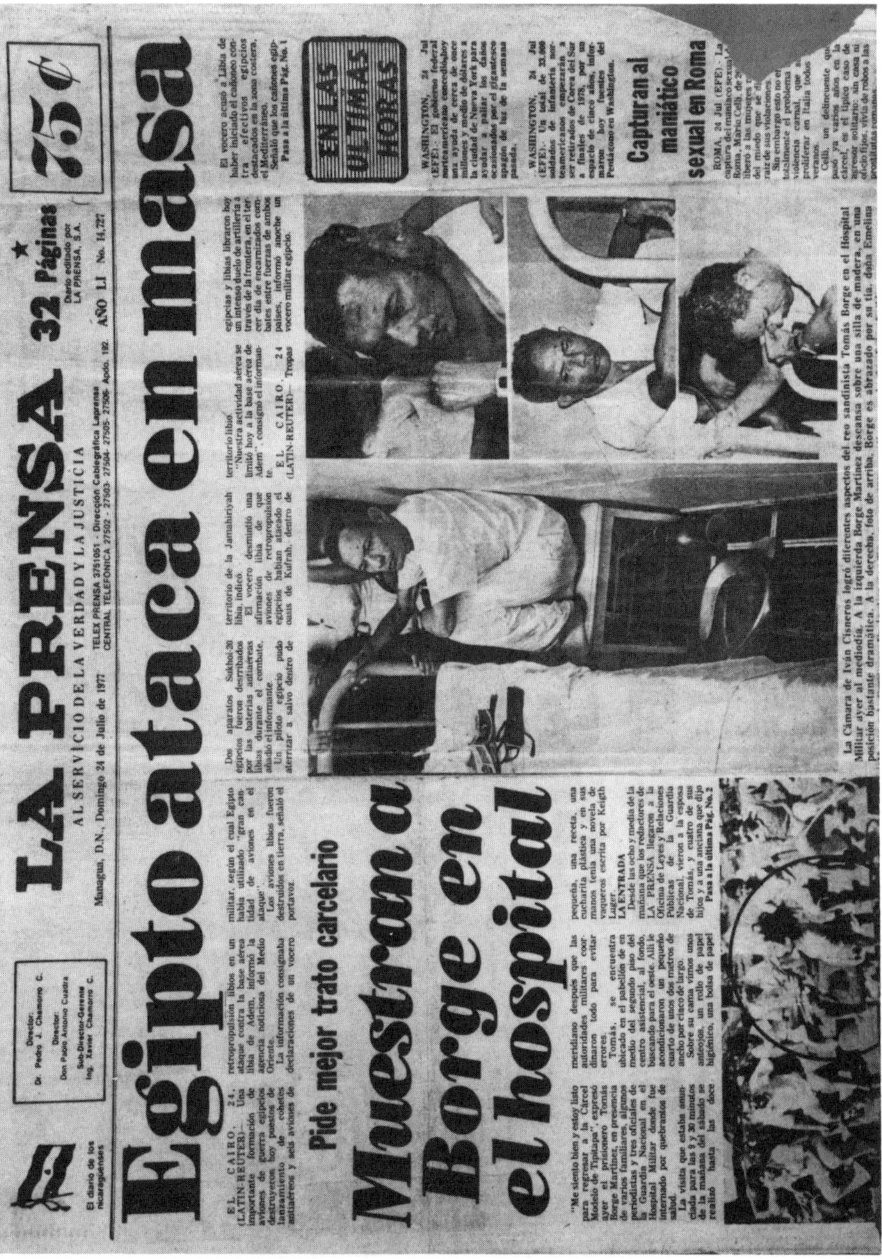

El diario de los nicaragüenses

Director: Dr. Pedro J. Chamorro C.
Director: Don Pablo Antonio Cuadra
Sub-Director-Gerente Ing. Xavier Chamorro C.

LA PRENSA

AL SERVICIO DE LA VERDAD Y LA JUSTICIA

32 Páginas ★ Diario editado por LA PRENSA, S.A.

75¢

Managua, D.N., Domingo 24 de Julio de 1977 — TELEX PRENSA 3751051 - Dirección Cablegráfica Laprensa — CENTRAL TELEFONICA 27502 - 27503- 27504- 27505- 27506- Apdo. 192. — AÑO LI No. 14,727

Egipto ataca en masa

EL CAIRO, 24, (LATIN-REUTER)— Una importante formación de aviones de guerra egipcios destruyeron hoy puestos de lanzamiento de cohetes antiaéreos y seis aviones de retropropulsión libios en un ataque contra la base aérea libia de Adem, informó la agencia noticiosa del Medio Oriente.

La información consignaba declaraciones de un vocero militar, según el cual Egipto había utilizado "gran cantidad de aviones en el ataque".

Los aviones libios fueron destruidos en tierra, señaló el portavoz.

Dos aparatos Sukhoi-20 egipcios fueron desrribados por las baterías antiaéreas libias durante el combate, añadió el informante.

Un piloto egipcio pudo aterrizar a salvo dentro de territorio de la Jamahiriyah libia, indicó.

El vocero desmintió una afirmación libia de que aviones de retropropulsión egipcios habían atacado el oasis de Kufrah, dentro de territorio libio.

"Nuestra actividad aérea se limitó hoy a la base aérea de Adem", consignó el informante.

EL CAIRO, 24 (LATIN-REUTER)— Tropas egipcias y libias libraron hoy un intenso duelo de artillería a través de la frontera, en el tercer día de encarnizados combates entre fuerzas de ambos países, informó anoche un vocero militar egipcio.

El vocero acusó a Libia de haber iniciado el cañoneo contra efectivos egipcios destacados en la zona costera, el Mediterráneo.

Señaló que los cañones egip-

Pasa a la última Pág. No. 1

Pide mejor trato carcelario

Muestran a Borge en el hospital

"Me siento bien y estoy listo para regresar a la Cárcel Modelo de Tipitapa", expresó ayer el prisionero Tomás Borge Martínez, en presencia de varios familiares, algunos periodistas y tres oficiales de la Guardia Nacional en el Hospital Militar donde fue internado por quebrantos de salud.

La visita que estaba anunciada para las 9 y 30 minutos de la mañana del sábado se realizó hasta las doce meridiano después que las autoridades militares coordinaron todo para evitar errores.

Tomás, se encuentra ubicado en el pabellón de en medio del segundo piso del centro asistencial, al fondo, buscando para el oeste. Allí le acondicionaron un pequeño cuarto de unos dos metros de ancho por cinco de largo.

Sobre su cama vimos unos anteojos, un rollo de papel higiénico, una bolsa de papel pequeña, una receta, una cucharita plástica y en sus manos tenía una novela de vaqueros escrita por Keigth Luger.

LA ENTRADA

Desde las ocho y media de la mañana que los redactores de LA PRENSA llegaron a la Oficina de Leyes y Relaciones Públicas de la Guardia Nacional, vieron a la esposa de Tomás, y cuatro de sus hijos y a una anciana que dijo

Pasa a la última Pág. No. 2

La Cámara de Iván Cisneros logró diferentes aspectos del reo sandinista Tomás Borge en el Hospital Militar ayer al mediodía. A la izquierda Borge Martínez descansa sobre una silla de madera, en una posición bastante dramática. A la derecha, foto de arriba, Borge es abrazado por su tía, doña Emelina

EN LAS ULTIMAS HORAS

WASHINGTON, 24 Jul (EFE).- El gobierno federal norteamericano concedió hoy una ayuda de cerca de once millones y medio de dólares a la ciudad de Nueva York para ayudar a paliar los daños ocasionados por el gigantesco apagón de luz de la semana pasada.

WASHINGTON, 24 Jul (EFE).- Un total de 33.000 soldados de infantería norteamericanos empezarán a ser retirados de Corea del Sur a finales de 1978, por un espacio de cinco años, informaron hoy fuentes del Pentágono en Washington.

Capturan al maniático sexual en Roma

ROMA, 24 Jul (EFE).- La captura del maniaco sexual de Roma, Mario Celli, de 2[illegible] liberó a las mujeres [illegible] del miedo que se [illegible] raíz de sus violaciones.

Sin embargo esto no e[illegible] totalmente el problema [illegible] violencia carnal, que [illegible] proliferar en Italia todos [illegible] veranos.

Celli, un delincuente qu[illegible] pasó ya varios años en la cárcel, es el típico caso de agresor solitario: sin casa ni oficio fijos, vivía de robos a las prostitutas romanas.

Front page *La Prensa* account of Borge's confinement in military hospital, July 1977.

FROM THE MODEL PRISON

A Personal Account of Incarceration.[1]

One Tuesday afternoon they took me from my cell. A police van was waiting near the main entrance. The officer on duty signaled for me to get in and before I could say a word they slammed the door shut behind me. I understood: they were taking me to the Military Hospital. Thus began one more episode in the difficult hunger strike I had initiated 50 days earlier to protest the inhuman, solitary confinement within a miniscule cell to which I have been subjected for the past 18 months.

The van speeds along the Northern Highway, closely escorted by several BECAT vehicles.[2] I drag myself forward to get a look out. Twilight is approaching with its clear, intense hues. Leaving behind the "Las Mercedes" residential complex, I see people leaving their jobs, waiting at bus stops or hurrying homeward. Young couples in love hold hands, look into each other's eyes and smile. At one point a ragged, barefoot boy runs by, seconds before the squeal of brakes and a loud curse. A fat old man waves to a girl wearing too much make-up. There is a scuffle on the corner off to the left, by the "La Esperanza" pharmacy. A quarrel, perhaps, or maybe an accident; traffic is heavy. I devour these moments filled with human faces and street sounds. I desperately want to hear voices, a single phrase — just one — that is undefiled by hate and arrogance. Beyond the train station the city's wounds remain untouched and open. The ruins of the Banco de América and the Intercontinental Hotel slip by in succession. In the waiting room at the Military Hospital we are met by Coronel Castellón. They rush me to a tiny, windowless room. The door down the hall — with opaque, taciturn panes — is nailed shut with heavy planks. A man with his face hidden behind a cloth mask and a penetrating voice characteristic of people who hide their faces behind cloth masks orders me to lie down on a thick-mattressed bed with the unmistakable cradle or coffin shape all hospital beds have. In seconds I am naked and manacled to the bed frame. They dress me in white pajamas. A young man with the appearance of a physician and a newlywed approaches and, visibly blushing, says to me:

"I have orders to give you an I.V. I beg you not to make this situation any more difficult than it is. If you resist, they're going to restrain you and put you to sleep."

A male nurse injects a white fluid into my hip and minutes later I drowsily feel the hypodermic needle entering my vein. I am suddenly conscious of an intense light, almost a spotlight, raining down like fire from the ceiling and illuminating the bare walls. I'm restless and violently move my arm. Shortly afterward the male nurse is back.

"The needle came out," he said "We'll have no alternative but to tie you down." I lie still and they don't tie me down. As though hypnotized I observe the droplets of serum falling sadly, slowly. I feel lethargic, but the spotlight, the heat and that indescribable discomfort won't let me sleep.

Hours later, around midnight, a man's authoritarian voice comes in through the doorway leading to the hallway.

"You lie still for me," he shouts. "Don't turn your head for even a second, ya hear me, scumbucket?"

"Yeah, I heard you," I reply without concealing my anger. "I'm not deaf, and I haven't the slightest desire to see your face."

"Don't think I'm afraid of you, motherfucker," he says to me as I hear his footsteps approach. I hear the sound of the handcuff closing. The steel digs into my flesh but I don't complain.

When the sunlight penetrates the opaque panes in the sealed door, I see the silhouette of a soldier with a submachine gun pacing back and forth on the other side. The I.V. bottle is nearly empty. The male nurse shuts the valve and the droplets stop falling. He doesn't remove the needle and I give him a questioning look. They turn off the light. It's daytime. A boy approaches carrying an appetizing breakfast tray. I refuse it. A little later the doctor arrives. I recognize him. It's Dr. López, a forensic specialist. I complain of the discomfort from the cruel combination of manacles, I.V., the spotlight, the heat, the hostility, and the prohibition of looking behind me. (Is it my relationship with Lot's family, doctor?) The forensic specialist says he understands, but that in order for him to help me I must eat.

Much later that day they open the I.V. valve and just when I think I'm finally going to get some rest, they leave the needle in and hang another bottle. God, am I naive! I didn't know it at the time but, naturally, we had scarcely begun. The hostility grows on invisible faces.

"This man urinates all the time. Tell him to stop being such a pain in the ass."

"It's the I.V.," explains the male nurse. "It makes you want to urinate every little while."

"So? I give a shit. Tell him not to piss, that's all!"

Another bottle: this one's a yellow color. Then a reddish one. The one after that is white. An intramuscular injection. They close and open the I.V. valve. They leave me alone and I rest briefly. I sit up and manage to read the medical label on the bottle: "Patient: Special Room" (I have no humor left to laugh at this original euphemism). "Pathology: Dehydration. Treatment: Dextrose" (and other illegible words).

Farther down I seem to make out the word Prednisone. I vaguely remembered the name of a hormone to combat arthritis, to stimulate the appetite and . . . Stimulate the appetite? I'm not sure, though, that that chemical product was actually written on the label. But the red liquid is surely Vitimin B complex. And then there are the appetizing dishes and . . .

"Eat." It's the sweet voice of a nurse with hair the color of old gold.

"Eat." It's the threatening voice of the invisible face.

"Eat." It's the neutral, professional voice of the male nurse.

"Eat, eat, eat . . ."

"Ah, he doesn't want to eat," comes a voice in the corridor. "What he needs is a bullet in the heart . . . Run that up through the window." (What could it be? Come on, don't give in to fear.) "Full throttle, and when you cross the street . . ."

Blackmail . . . "Let the animal die once and for all . . ." Handclaps.

Words that light up, vials that turn off, cold sweat, hunger . . . I'm hungry! No. I won't eat. I won't eat that plate of chopped meat, the splendorous rice, the fresh slices of tomato. I won't.

Intramuscular red liquid, my arms and buttocks are inflamed, Prednisone, the needle in my vein, the cold, humiliating manacle on my wrist, the hot air, my shoulders ache, the mattress is an oven, my relationship to Lot's family, please give me some air, the light that pierces my closed eyes, pass me the pitcher, you're a pain in the ass, the droplets fall slowly, softly like feline footsteps in the night, what unbearable suffering, I'm hungry, my God, I'm hungry!

Green serum, red serum, yellow serum, white, one day, two days, three days. An officer appears. He's in civilian clothes but the agents call him "Sir".

"What is it you demand, Tomás?" His voice is courteous, almost friendly. "We are interested in resolving your problem."

"For 18 months I've been in solitary confinement," I reply, "locked up in a cell 2 meters by 4 meters and discriminated against. I am allowed barely an hour and a half, and sometimes only an hour, each week for visitors. The rest of the week I'm not permitted even to speak to anyone. I've asked myself many times what is the reason for this cruel treatment and the only answer I've been able to find is that you want to drown me in a pool of hatred and rancor. I'm an honest man. I recognize that the treatment accorded the other Sandinista prisoners is fairly acceptable, given the conditions of this country. But in my case and that of Marcio Jaén an exception has been made that I find unacceptable. Remember that the so-called Human Rights are a matter of common sense, rather than of generosity or of sadism. You have Marcio in solitary confinement, despite the fact that the boy was only given a 5-year prison sentence, for the sole purpose of not focusing public attention on my particular case. You have sacrificed Marcio in order to satiate your rage against me. I demand an end to our solitary confinement and that we not be forced to suffer additional punishments that would be considered illegal and inhuman in any country in the world."

The officer was thoughtful for a moment and then said: "It's not within my power to solve your problem. I assure you, however, that in my judgment your demands do not seem unreasonable and that there is almost a one hundred percent probability that they will be met. Nevertheless, the first step you must take as a show of good faith and as a sign that your hunger strike has no political ends is to eat. You can be sure that once you have recovered and return to the Model Prison, you will find a fair and reasonable response to your demands."

Another four days with the I.V., the heat, the handcuffs, the hostility. Hunger has turned into a desperate anxiety. Five days, six days. The suffering is unbearable. My blood pressure drops to dangerous levels. They take my blood pressure every two hours. A group of submachine-gun-toting officers led by a captain arrived "to meet me", their attitude menacing. They promised to pay me another visit.

The seventh day: "I'm going to remove your handcuffs and the I.V. so you can rest," says someone with a whispery, persuasive voice. "They're going to bathe and shave you."

They bathe me and shave me. I'm very weak. The individual with the whispery, persuasive voice comes up behind me.

"This is chicken. He passes the plate under my nose and the delicious fragrance convulses my innards. "We prepared it especially for you, pal."

I feel my resolve weakening. So many days without eating. I have suffered so much. No one can say you're weak, that you don't keep your promises. Human resistance has its limits. Besides, they have promised to resolve the prison problem and the hunger strike is not an end in itself. What would you say, my love? You who believe I'm strong . . . If you eat they'll turn out the light, they'll let you urinate in peace, perhaps they'll remove the cuffs, maybe they'll even allow family visits. Oh, Mama, just a little rest. You can die and there'll still be a world to build in what is now a lake of saliva, this circle of fangs. No, my brothers, no, my love, I will not eat. That's not chicken, it's the flesh of an old drunkard who died of syphilis. Look at it: it's the skin of his rotting arms. The promises they make you are false. It's certain that solidarity is growing now both in the country and abroad. Hunger is infinite, but where is your strength? You can die, to be sure, but who has told you that you're indispensable? Carlos died, honest, generous, agile-minded Carlos. The one who saw further than any of us. Why aren't you going to die, you who have called yourself his disciple?

But if . . . maybe everything's already settled. They know that if they continue with the solitary confinement, with the brutal discrimination, you're not going to resign yourself to it. No one would. The demands, the protests, the international condemnation will all continue. Nor are they unaware that should they move you back with your comrades, nothing will happen. On the contrary, everything would remain tranquil. Acceding to a demand does not diminish the principle of authority. Perhaps they've finally understood that.

The individual with the whispery, persuasive voice insists: "You must eat. Do you want to die?"

There's a remedy for everything except death. Your comrades await you. Your family is suffering on your account. At bottom, your attitude is vain and egotistical. You think only of yourself, you've forgotten your loved ones. And for what? So people will say you're a hero. Let's be practical. The aim of the hunger strike is to improve your situation. That has now been accomplished. Why, then, should you keep on suffering? The whispery, persuasive voice filters through my viscera. I have a desire to slap him, to shake his hand, to cry. "The sun shines for everyone and I assure you that it will continue to shine for you, too. Tonight they will turn out the light for you. We will remove the handcuffs as long as you have the I.V. If you eat, of course, the I.V. will no longer be required."

He places the dish under my nose. Next to the meat is a resplendent portion of rice, toast, butter, and what appears to be an apple pastry.

"Are you certain," I ask, "that there has been some kind of response to my situation in the Model Prison?"

"I'm not in a position to answer that, but it's almost certain."

"All right. Leave the plate on the chair."

There is dead silence. The individual with the whispery, persuasive voice withdraws. Behind my back I hear his voice addressing another invisible face in a different tone.

"He's eating."

In the corridor there is a cruel, cutting laugh.

EPILOGUE

They gave me 32,000 cc of serum and tens of intramuscular injections. Manacled they take me back to Tipitapa Prison — which they have renamed the Model Prison. Once again I see the street. I don't know why I now feel an infinite tenderness toward the men, women and children who walk along the sidewalks, wait for buses, love, laugh and suffer oblivious to my own tragedy. They, too, I think, have their tragedies, albeit on a different plane. How I love them!

Back in prison I remain in solitary confinement, serving in my solitude. Marcio, too. I am not, however, resigned to it. I shall never resign myself to it. Do they understand?

TOMAS BORGE
29 July, 1977
Model Prison, Tipitapa

Borge with 12-year-old daughter, Ana Josefina, May 1987

LETTER TO ANA JOSEFINA

12 April 1977

Ana Josefina:
Today, on your second birthday, your father recalls with particular intensity that moment of love when, together with your mother, it was decided to bring you into this life. This means, little one, that you were not born by chance or accident. I even recall the day your life began. Your mother and I shared emotion and joy — it was a mild August night — for we were certain the miracle had happened.

Afterward, as you grew day by day within your mother's body, we waited eagerly to enjoy your first movements. The day you arrived — April 12, 1975 — they tried to kill me. But that day was so filled with your presence that there was no room for death. When you were 10 months old, I fell into the hands of the enemies of our people. They beat me brutally; hooded and manacled for 9 months, I clung to your memory, to the imperative need to be worthy of my people so that I might be worthy of you. Had I fallen to my knees before them, I would be the first to ask that you forsake me. But I was and shall remain loyal to my principles.

One of my deepest desires is that you be proud of me. The few merits I possess to earn that pride, however, are not and never will be equal to those of your mother, who is the most loving and honest of women. When you were a newborn infant, she washed your clandestine diapers until she was exhausted; she lived, and lives, entirely devoted to you and to me. When you're grown up, though I shall thirst for your love, you must above all else reserve a very special place for your mother. This must never come into conflict with any other duty. If you are generous, if in your heart there is no room for egotism, if you confront injustice with passion and courage, then that beautiful moment when your mother and I became one flesh to initiate your life will have justified the flame we desired to light.

Your father,
Tomás

PRISON POEMS AND OTHER POETRY

LA CEREMONIA ESPERADA

Fuí al encuentro con la jauría
de los rateros de polen
para dilucidar el antiguo estilo del sol
y en la alterna claridad
fue posible saber
que el escalofrío
la idiosincracia de los ángulos
el irrenunciable malestar de la miel
la honestidad de la magia
estaban exactamente en el rostro
que moviéndose hacia atrás
se acercaba a mis ojos recuperados
y el costado sur de la rodilla
identificado por una luz tenue
irreprochable
hasta que aceptó cierto grado de calor
el inicio de la ceremonia esperada.

23 de julio de 1973

THE AWAITED CEREMONY

I went to face the pack
of pollen thieves
to decipher the ancient form of the sun
and in the alternate clarity
was able to see
that the shudder
the idiosyncracy of angels
the irrenounceable disquiet of honey
the honesty of that magic
were concentrated in your face
which turning back
drew nearer to my restored sight
and the southern side of your knee
illuminated by a tenuous glow
lay beyond reproach
until sufficient warmth came
to initiate the awaited ceremony.

23 July 1973

ENCUENTRO

Ya tus perfumes en mi sangre
ya tus manos en mis manos
ya tus ojos no ven los nuestros
ya las palabras depositadas en el
suspiro de los leopardos
el breve cinturón café
el brasier
los detalles ocultos que florecen
cuando despejamos la soledad
las caricias que nunca se saben si son
las tuyas o las mías
este olor a playa a musgo a recorrido
la música la lluvia la tormenta
ya la ternura se mueve
¡Ay los suspiros amplios!
¡Ya un escalofrío tuyo!
¡Ay corren por la sangre,
amor, ya!

mayo de 1977

ENCOUNTER

Your scents now merged in my blood
your hands now in my hands
your eyes no longer seeing our eyes
our words now deposited
in the leopard's sighs
your short coffee-colored belt
your brassiere
hidden details that flower
as we dispel solitude
caresses that are indistinguishable
yours from mine
this aroma of beach, moss, familiar path
the music, the rain, the storm
now tenderness stirs
Oh, the fullness of our sighs!
Now a shivering within you!
Oh love, in our blood,
now!

May 1977

CASI TODO

Todo sobra
el orín de los ángeles
cabalgando en sus alfileres
los basureros sobran
o sea los jardines
la entrega de las amapolas
cuando apenas eso tiene
la importancia de una abeja,
el irreprochable sacrificio
de las cintas adhesivas
el ruido
sus alternativas
el timbre del teléfono
que anuncia los insoslayables
casi todo
basta una sola de tus manos
el corto circuito que circula en el bordado
el estilo
basta

junio de 1977

ALMOST EVERYTHING

Everything's in excess
the urine of the angels
galloping on their pinheads
refuse heaps are in excess
which is to say gardens
the offering of poppies
when that's scarcely
more relevant than a honey bee
the irreproachable sacrifice
of adhesive tape
noise
its alternatives
the telephone's ring
announcing the inevitable
almost everything
one of your hands alone is enough
the short circuit running through the embroidery
style
is enough

June 1977

¿QUE HARAS?

Amor, hay algo en el recuerdo
que es un violín por la noche
son las 11
a esta hora
mis manos se comen
las luces atrapadas
que dejaron tus ojos
¿Qué harás?

julio de 1977

WHAT ARE YOU DOING NOW?

Love, there's something in my memory
a violin piercing the night
It's 11 o'clock
at this hour
my hands devour
the trapped lights
left behind by your eyes
What are you doing now?

July 1977

LA QUE MASTICA SUEÑOS

Es una muchacha
de corazón brusco
que metió en el lugar exacto
sus raíces de gata
es una muchacha de 29 años
heterogénea, dragón
que mastica sueños
y cristales empañados
es una muchacha
que rasca
la superficie del sol
mientras ahorca
objetivos intermedios
es llovizna
área verde
expresión

julio de 1977

THE GIRL WHO CHEWS UP DREAMS

She's a girl
of abrupt heart
who in the precise place sank
her cat-like roots
she's a girl of 29
heterogeneous, a dragon
who chews up dreams
and tarnished crystals
she's a girl
who scratches
the surface of the sun
while strangling
lesser objectives
she is soft rain
green expanse
expression

July 1977

NICARAGUA

Te amo desde aquí, volcán
tinaja quebrada
canoa entre peces antropófagos

Desde mi soledad te amo
torbellino, espejo
apaleado en el valle de los estruendos

Amo los muslos lineales
de tus ojos enseñado los dientes
llorando pirotecnia
amo tus poetas famosos y tristes
tus muertos alegres
que se niegan a morir.

13 de agosto de 1977

NICARAGUA

I love you from here, volcano
cracked vase of clay
canoe amidst flesh-eating fish

From my loneliness I love you
whirlwind, mirror
bashed in the valley of thunder

I love the lineal thighs
of your eyes baring teeth
weeping pyrotecnics
I love your poets, famous and sad
your joyful dead
who refuse to die.

13 August 1977

YA NO

¿Has visto una cortina roja
en mi fatigada alcoba?
¿Has bebido sombra
cuando los labios están secos?
¿Has metido las manos
entre las rodillas
cuando las hojas oscuras
tienen frío?

Es preciso conocer el frío
para amar el calor
y la compañía es una opción
cuando la soledad nos golpeó
con su martillo negro
yo estaré tan solo
como sea necesario
pero ya no tanto

agosto de 1977

NO MORE

Have you seen a red curtain
in my weary chamber?
Have you drunk shadows
when your lips are parched?
Have you sunk your hands
between your knees
when the dark leaves
are cold?

One must know cold
to love warmth
and companionship is an option
when loneliness has struck us
with its black hammer
I shall be as alone
as I must
but never again so alone.

August 1977

A PROPOSITO DE UN LENGUAJE IRRESPETUOSO

La herencia de los cuchillos
no viene de las Segovias, señor,
los perros ladran
— Ud. ser la hija de Pedrón
— Soy la hija del General Pedro Altamirano
gringo hijuelagranputa

En el tapesco hay cápsulas vacías y flores rojas,
señor.

agosto de 1977

APROPOS OF DISRESPECTFUL SPEECH

Our legacy of knives, sir,
doesn't come from the Segovias,
dogs bark
"Ain't you Pedrón's daughter?"
"I'm the daughter of General Pedro Altamirano,[1]
gringo son-of-a-bitch"

In our humble shelter there are empty cartridges and
red flowers,
sir.

August 1977

A PROPOSITO DEL DISCURSO DE UN DIPUTADO SOMOCISTA

¿Hijos de la misma patria?
Ustedes esbirros, ustedes honorables
ustedes, ratas
excelencias
Ustedes y nosotros
nacimos en una sola geografía
bajo las mismas estrellas
es igualita la luna lampiña
que rescató de amarillo
nuestros primeros sueños.

Hay aproximadamente, una idéntica ración de calor
en nuestras respectivas cuotas de sol y de raíces
sin duda somos hijos de nuestras madres
pero no somos hijos de la misma patria.

septiembre de 1977

APROPOS OF A SPEECH BY A SOMOCISTA CONGRESSMAN

Sons of the same fatherland?
You thugs, you honorable ones
you, vermin
excellencies
You and we
were born in a single geography
beneath the same stars
the beardless moon
that saved our earliest dreams from yellowing
is one and the same.

There is, approximately, an identical ration of warmth
in our respective quotas of sun and roots
without a doubt we are our mother's sons
but we are not sons of the same fatherland.

September 1977

LA PIEDRA

Para recuperar tu piedra, Andrés,
hace falta algo más
que un poco de paciencia
sin duda no la fatigada
cara de los aniversarios
ni el recuento de las intransigencias
menos la regurgitación de las palabras
tu piedra sigue, Andrés,
intacta, en algún lugar próximo,
es un fragmento de la calle
es la conciencia
a lo mejor está en Monimbó, en el Ocote
tal vez en el repliegue del arco iris.
Seguro.

septiembre de 1977

THE STONE

To recover your stone, Andrés,[2]
something more is needed
than mere patience
certainly not the tired
face of our anniversaries
nor the retelling of our intransigencies[3]
still less the regurgitation of words
your stone, Andrés, remains
intact, in some nearby place
it is a fragment of the street
it is conscience
it may be in Monimbó, or Ocote
perhaps in the retreat of the rainbow.[4]
I'm sure of it.

September 1977

CUMPLEAÑOS

Hoy es un día, cariño,
que saldrá a la calle uniformado
repicando estampillas
sudando el borde de las muescas
bajo sus minutos fatigados
pasarán los burócratas,
las monedas, sin duda,
levantarán las patitas
para orinar la orilla del sol
los niños en las escuelas correrán detrás de sus risas
el llanto brusco de cualquiera será un adiós
o algo menos importante.
Cuantas cosas
nos tomaremos las manos
me besarás
diré que te quiero
con un tono tal vez de aniversario
no te daré flores
ni blusas estampadas
ni un ajedrez con peones amarillos;
sólo
que hoy, ayer, mañana y siempre es hoy.

5 de noviembre de 1977

BIRTHDAY

Today's a day, sweetheart,
that'll step uniformed into the street
bureaucrats will pass by
beneath their tired minutes
licking stamps
their collars tinged with sweat
coins will doubtless
raise their tiny legs
to urinate at the sun's edge
school children will chase after their laughter
sudden tears will signify a parting
or something less momentous.
So many things
we'll hold hands
you will kiss me
I'll say I love you
as if, perhaps, it were our anniversary
I won't give you flowers
nor print blouses
nor a chess set with yellow pawns;
only
that today, yesterday, tomorrow and forever is today.

5 November 1977

LA SALIDA DEL SOL

Noviembre es el amanecer
sale un sol en el oeste
sale un sol en el norte
sale un sol en el este
sale un sol en el sur
yo nací en Noviembre
y volví a nacer en Noviembre
ya murió la angustia
sólo quedó el amor
Noviembre es el mes de nuestro amor

noviembre de 1977

SUNRISE

November is the dawn
a sun rises in the West
a sun rises in the North
a sun rises in the East
a sun rises in the South
I was born in November
and was reborn in November
anguish has died
only love remains
November is the month of our love

November 1977

CUANDO NO ESTAS

Carencia de mariposas
aquí no hay arena
cielo no hay
obstetricia de colillas apagadas
desfile de agujeros

El día es carne carbonizada
crepúsculo al borde del sarcasmo
todos los colores y perfumes
se fueron en tu piel

noviembre de 1977

WHEN YOU'RE NOT HERE

Absence of butterflies
here there is no sand
no sky
obstetrics of snuffed-out cigarettes
a parade of empty holes

The day is burnt flesh
twilight at sarcasm's edge
every hue and scent
has fled upon your skin

November 1977

NACIMIENTO

Los meses
son un amanecer
nuestra vida es la hora
cualquier día es un aniversario
Octubre sale como un sol en el norte
Diciembre aparece en el oeste
hoy y hace 24 días
el lunes a las 14 horas
nacieron sonrisas
reproches, caricias.
Esta vida es la hora de los partos.

diciembre de 1977

BIRTH

The months
are but a dawn
our life a single hour
any day is an anniversary
October rises like a sun in the North
December appears in the West
today and 24 days ago
Monday at 2 pm
were born smiles
reproaches, caresses.
This life is the hour of birthing.

December 1977

LAMPARA

Sos un lingote de lluvia que salta
de piedra en flor
exactamente igual que el resplandor de
los tomates
una cuerda tendida
desde el alquitrán
            ese paraíso
donde se apagaron los altavoces
    dos
    tres
    cuatro
    sin=
    cuenta
    lámparas
el permiso otorgado por el sol
para averiguar mi sombra

1977

LAMP

You're an ingot of rain that leaps
from rock to flower
identical to the tomato's
luster
a life line leading
from the tar
            that paradise
where the loudspeakers have been silenced
      two
      three
      four
      count=
      less
      lamps
permission granted by the sun
to ascertain my own shadow

1977

VISITA EN LA CARCEL

Como en la sangre
como el perfil del gato
igual que la riña solidaria del sol
con la clorofila en los cascos
de los caballos frescos
dame, amor, el paso alegre de tus sandalias de bronce,
el paso triste de tus zapatos de espuma
dame tu boca lenta
la descarada luna de tus rodillas de arena
la cintura en dígito
— esa amenaza de trapecio y de legumbre —
el agua en la espada para acariciar
la risa, alimento, las manos, las palabras,
la limpia, sí, la dulce piedra.

mayo de 1978

JAIL VISIT

As in the blood
like a cat's silhouette
same as the sun's solidary quarrel
with the chlorophyll on the hooves
of fresh horses
give me, love, the joyful step of your bronze sandals,
the sad step of your foam shoes
give me your unhurried mouth
the faceless moon of your knees of sand
your digital waist
— that menace of trapeze and seed —
water on the sword to caress
your laughter, sustenance, hands, words,
the pure, yes, the sweet stone.

May 1978

VERANO

Desde la ventana
la lluvia es un río en posición de firme
que golpea el inútil esfuerzo del sol
¡pobre hormiga orinando sobre el incendio!
No hay amor, invierno
aunque en las charcas
naden temblorosas las estrellas
o la fatiga se ensucie de tinieblas
o las lágrimas repitan la vieja contraseña
Es inútil;
no hay invierno

1978

SUMMER

From my window
the rain is a river standing at attention
against which the sun beats to no avail
poor ant urinating on the fire!
There is no love, no winter
even though shimmering stars
swim in the puddles
or weariness soils itself in darkness
or tears recite the old password
It's no use;
there is no winter.

1978

LA INSTANTANEA

Levantó vuelo la mariposa
desde que llegaste, amiga,
con la cintura dispuesta a la brevedad
y al fruto de tu vientre, amén.
Excesivamente bruja, excesivamente maga.
Premonición de Valeria,
la rodilla apenas sugerida
deliberadamente luna y excesiva,
los pezones obviamente vanguardia
de un doble resplandor,
las palabras organizadas en pretérito
con la sospecha del violín
en la yema de los dedos.
Desde que llegaste, amor,
se ejerció sobre la silueta
la dictadura del arcoiris.
Se rompió el reloj;
fue una instantánea.

1985

SNAPSHOT

The butterfly has taken flight
since you arrived, dear friend,
with your waist tending toward brevity
and the fruit of your womb, amen.
Excessively bewitching, excessively magical.
Premonition of Valeria,[5]
the bare suggestion of your knee
deliberately, excessively moon-like,
your nipples manifestly the vanguard
of a double radiance,
your words arranged in past tense
with a hint of violin
on your fingertips.
Since you arrived, love,
the dictatorship of the rainbow
has imposed itself on your silhouette.
The clock has shattered;
it was all in a snapshot.

1985

ME ENTREGASTE UN GOLPE DE RUISEÑOR

Me entregaste un golpe de ruiseñor, amiga,
y lo lancé con fuerza.
Se fue.
Se hizo nave y desde sus ventanas
se asomó al universo.
Pero ¡ay! era sólo un golpe de ruiseñor

1986

YOU GAVE ME THE JOLT OF A NIGHTINGALE[6]

You gave me the jolt of a nightingale, dear lady,
and I propelled it powerfully.
It rose
became a ship and from its windows
gazed out upon the universe.
Alas! It was only the jolt of a nightingale.

1986

REPRESION

Ordeno, es decir, ruego,
que las tardes opacas
se conviertan en fósforo,
arrebatar el polen
para que su vino
embriague a los tractores
Ordeno condenar a las estrellas
sólo cuando estén bordadas
como rayas de leopardo;

Suscribir un protocolo
con Ernesto Cardenal
sobre la liberación de los potros
y el internacionalismo de los pájaros
y la pena de muerte y el indulto
de los cisnes y sátiros.

Ordeno atacar los flancos de la retórica
reconocer el maíz y el derecho del pastizal
a convertirse en bandera
no considerar la frase de Armstrong
como inmortal.
Identificar al enemigo
agazapado en el muro
de los lugares comunes,
y transformar la realidad
y, por tanto,
la incidencia de las legumbres;

Ordeno bañar con clorofilo el horrendo dictamen de Séneca.
No todo es gusano.
Condenar a cadena perpetua las sombras
por su vieja conspiración contra los niños.

REPRESSION

I order, which is to say, I beseech
that opaque afternoons
turn phosphorescent,
that pollen be captured
so that its wine
might intoxicate the tractors.
I order condemnation of the stars
only when they are embroidered
like leopard's stripes;

That a protocol be signed
with Ernesto Cardenal
on the liberation of young horses
and the internationalism of birds
and the death penalty and pardon
of the swans and the satyrs.

I order an attack on rhetoric's flanks,
that maize be acknowledged, together with the right
of pastureland to be raised as a banner,
that Armstrong's words
not be considered immortal.
That the enemy be identified
crouching behind the wall
of common places,
and that reality be transformed
and with it, the abundance of beans.

I order that Seneca's horrendous verdict be cleansed with
chlorophyll.
Not all is worm-eaten.
Let the shadows be incarcerated
for their age-old conspiracy against children.

Ordeno que Hera deje de ser hormiga
y con Cronos convertido en caballo
puedan hacer el amor.

Ordeno el respeto de los semáforos,
aunque el color rojo hay que respetarlo
por otras razones; traer al recinto
los besos que nos damos
en este río profündo y transparente,
en esta ciudad del sol
que es también la ciudad de la luna
y de las consignas en plural,
y del olvido de Sigfrido;

Ordeno, es decir, ruego,
fuego rasante contra la resignación y el colesterol
y que la Flor de Loto Azul despliegue sus vainas
preciosas como una muralla
para vencer la espada del Dios Amarillo
con cara de pavo real de un solo ojo
cagado, prepotente y triste;

Ordeno la reencarnación de la utopía
y recuperar la memoria del bohemio
hermoso y terrible.

Yo soy tu hermano lobo.
La vida no es ironía, ni disculpa
ni siquiera falta de respeto.

Es la antigua deflagración, amigo,
por la que estamos dispuestos
a entregar la piel.

I order that Hera cease being an ant
and together with Cronus turned stallion,
be permitted to make love.

I order that traffic lights be respected,
although the color red should be respected
for other reasons; that
the kisses we share
in this deep and transparent river,
in this city of the sun
which is also the city of the moon
and of slogans in chorus
and of the forgetfulness of Siegfried,
be brought into the station house.

I order, which is to say, I beseech
fire to rain on resignation and on cholesterol
and the Blue Lotus Flower to deploy its precious
sheaths like a rampart
to foil the sword of the Yellow God
with the face of a one-eyed peacock,
shit-covered, arrogant and sad;

I order the reincarnation of Utopia
and the recovery of the memory of that
beautiful and terrible Bohemian.

I am your brother wolf.
Life is neither irony nor apology
nor even lack of respect.

It's the age-old fire of purification, my friend,
for which we are prepared
to give up our skins.

Hay que dar a cada quien lo
que le pertenece, ordeno;
la carroña a los bizcos,
que ignoran que la dirección del agua
es el mar.

Ordeno el reproche y la muerte a la compulsión
que acapara el oro, el maquillaje
la insidia del pronombre personal;
Ordeno recuperar a Dionisio encerrado en
el muslo de Zeus,
prohibir la nostalgia,
el miedo y la dependencia tecnológica.

Distribuir el verano
a lo largo del invierno
y el invierno lucido
— el sueño de naranjas —
en los espacios de mi hermano Jaime.

Ordeno, es decir, ruego,
que este país, donde se terminó el susurro,
sea la república donde los caramelos
persigan a los niños.

1987

To each must be given
what is rightfully theirs, I order;
carrion for the cross-eyed who
don't know that water flows to the sea.

I order the censure and death of the compulsion
to hoard gold and cosmetics,
of the insidiousness of the personal pronoun;
I order the redemption of Dionysus, imprisoned
In Zeus' thigh,
the prohibition of nostalgia,
fear and technological dependency.

Let summer be dispersed
throughout the Winter
and the generous Winter
— dream of oranges —
over the dominions of my brother Jaime.[7]

I order, which is to say, I beseech
that this country, where whispering has ceased,
become the republic in which caramels
chase after the children.

1987

NO ESTOY

No estoy en tu rostro
Estoy en una península
oscura como el número seis
con dulzura íntima
y obsesivos ojos
interrogando algas

No estoy en tus rodillas
luciérnagas
dirigiendo
el golpe del zenzontle
Estoy tiritando al otro
lado de esta soledad
anís

No estoy en tus manos
Triste de este lado del Wankí estoy
con la boca llena de caballos
de niños que graban
sus huellas
en los acordes de la diosa Pasht

No estoy en la falanga del segundo dedo
Estoy entre niños curiosos
por mi ternura a prueba
de candalabros
hormigas
bocas despiadadas y corales

No estoy
en la cerradura azul
No estoy.

1988

I AM NOT

I am not in your countenance
I'm on a peninsula
dark as the number six
with intimate sweetness
and obsessive eyes
questioning seaweed

I am not in your knees
fireflies
homing
the mockingbird's peck
I'm trembling
on the far side
of this anise-flavored
solitude

I am not in your hands
Sadly I'm on this side of the River Wankí
my mouth full of horses
and children who inscribe
their marks
in the chords of the goddess Pasht

I am not in the bone of your index finger
I'm among curious children
out of a tenderness hardened against
candalabras
ants
cruel mouths and coral strings

I am not
in the blue lock
I'm not.

1988

LO TUYO, LO MIO

Lo tuyo es mi
lengua tuya

Lo mío es tu
palabra mía

Soy tu nave
sos mi río

Mi naranja es mi
pájaro tuyo

Tu azul es tu
baraja mía

Nuestros adverbios
son míos
son tuyos

1988

YOURS, MINE

Yours is my
tongue of yours

Mine is your
word of mine

I am your ship
you are my river

My orange is my
bird of yours

your blue is your
shuffled deck of mine

Our adverbs
are mine
are yours

1988

AHI ESTABA

Te ofrecí el arco iris
fue un error.
Estuve a punto de ofrecerte
un pájaro rojo
para abrir con su conjuro
la puerta
pero no logré atraparlo.

Busqué surtilegios
marfiles, dioses calcinados
para rastrear
tus huellas.

Nada encontré.
Busqué al final
el dulce estorbo
cerca de la tráquea
en dirección
al ventrículo izquierdo,
ahí estaba.

1988

THERE IT WAS

I offered you the rainbow
it was a mistake.
I was about to offer you
a red bird
to open the door
with his incantation
but I could not capture him.

I searched for spells
ivories, incinerated gods
to trace
your footsteps.

I found nothing.
At last I sought
the sweet impediment
near your trachea
close by
your left ventricle,
there it was.

1988

CHE

Si una vez más dividimos la historia
será desde aquel día de octubre
en que algunos aprendieron a temblar
a conocer que el fuego de los dioses
está en el corazón de los hombres
Resulta peligroso manosear las cenizas
cerrar los oídos al áspero
concierto de las guitarras

Nadie puede ocultar desde aquel día
que los muertos no se quedan callados
que empezaron a hablar sin que puedan
cortarles el uso de las rosas pardas
No hay duda que la hora de sus muertes
es una categoría en sí misma
la tierna renuncia
de los breves incendios

Aprendimos, che, que se puede ser
¿cómo se llama el caballero andante
el que llegó como un rey victorioso
el dulce vagabundo ocupado
a tiempo completo en resolver fantasías?
La gloria es sólo un cerillo que se rasga
en la retaguardia, y la vida hermosa
como el pezón de tu madre, como la milpa

Aprendimos, comandante, que nadie
puede consolarnos, porque quienes
nos pueden consolar necesitan consuelo
y porque, al fin y al cabo, lo que necesitamos

CHE

If yet again we divide history
it must be from that October day
when some learned to tremble
seeing that the fire of the gods
burns in the hearts of men.
It is dangerous to disturb the ashes,
to close your ears to the discordant
concert of guitars.

From that day forth no one can pretend
that the dead remain silent,
that they no longer speak out,
nor any longer have need of their drab roses.
Doubtless, the hour of their deaths
is a category unto itself,
the gentle renunciation
of short-lived fires.

We learned, Che, that it is possible to be--
what's the name of that wandering knight,
the one who arrived like a triumphant king,
that gentle vagabond consumed
with resolving fantasies?
Glory is but a match struck
behind the lines, and life's as beautiful
as your mother's nipple, as a plot of corn.

We learned, Major, that no one
can console us, for those who might
do so must themselves be consoled,
and after all is said and done, what we require

es otra cosa

cómo matar la muerte
cómo revivir la vida
cómo, carajo, utopicar

2 julio 1988

is something else--

How to kill death
how to resurrect life
how in hell to visualize utopia.

2 July 1988

LA DULCE CONDICION

Ya que no es posible
que vos y yo
viajemos las viente mil leguas
submarinas
visitemos el rostro oculto
de la luna
cumplamos el proyecto
histórico
de degollar cómplices
un millón de gorriones
tengamos una aventura
Ya que no es posible
buscar en la caverna
húmeda
referencias del ombligo
secreto
la dulce condición
a musgo
a abanico
a acorus calamus
a levedad
a homenaje a entretanto
a vértigo
Ya que no es posible
la uva cubriéndose
de estrellas derretidas
la calle unánime
confidencial
resplandeciente de fósforo
y música
tengamos una aventura
Dos o tres aventuras
Una aventura cuando

THE GENTLE CONDITION

Now that it's not possible
for you and me
to travel twenty thousand leagues
beneath the sea
let's visit the hidden face
of the moon.
Let's complete
the historic project
of conspiratorially beheading
a million sparrows.
Let's have an adventure
now that it's not possible
to seek in the humid cavern
references to
umbilical secrets.
The gentle condition
moss-like
fan-like
like aromatic sweet flag
levity
an homage to meanwhile
vertigo.
Now that it's not possible
— the grape covering itself
with dissolved starlight
the street unanimous
confidential
aglow with phosphorous
and music —
let's have an adventure.
Two or three adventures.
An adventure

haya noticia del viaje
de una nave espacial
hacia los agujeros negros
que son anaranjados
y que la pelota azul donde
habita mi amor
a prueba de dogmas
y relicarios
vuela hacia el jardín
izquierdo
más allá de la barrera
donde se rompe la nota
musical que compartimos
una aventura después
de que se cuele
furtiva
una metáfora de Verlaine
en el diálogo
de una vendedora de frutas
con media docena
de cinturas estrechas
Una aventura cuando
se apodere de nosotros
el miedo a la perfección
Entonces nos miraremos
de cerca
y tus ojos redondos
adquirirán el tamaño
de un jilguero
las horas se buscarán
de nuevo
como lunas crecientes
sin artificio
de dicha
No es lo que quiero
conste
pero es preferible

when there is news
of a space ship's journey
to the black holes,
which are orange,
and the blue ball on which
my love resides
protected from dogmas
and religious relics
hurtles leftward
toward the garden
beyond the barrier
where the musical
note we shared
is broken.
An adventure where
we slip a furtive
metaphor of Verlaine
into a fruit vendor's
conversation
along with a half dozen
narrow waists.
An adventure when
we are seized
by fear of perfection.
Then we'll look at each other
up close
and your round eyes
will become the size
of a goldfinch.
Once again
we'll seek hours
of happiness
like innocent waxing moons.
It is not what I want,
to be sure,
but it is preferable

a que el sol
se quede sin olfato
a morir un día
cercenado
como aquella rosa
que reparten los miserables
en los campos Elíseos
sobre la que ha caído
el estigma de Balzac
No es lo que quiero
vale
pero una aventura
dos tal vez
como los ojos de un venado
sorprendido en la noche

15 de octubre de 1988

to the sun
being denied
a sense of smell
or to the day dying
like that cut rose
shared by the wretched
of the Elysian Fields
upon which the stigma of Balzac
has fallen.
Indeed,
it's not this I want,
rather an adventure,
two perhaps,
like the eyes of a deer
surprised in the night.

15 October 1988

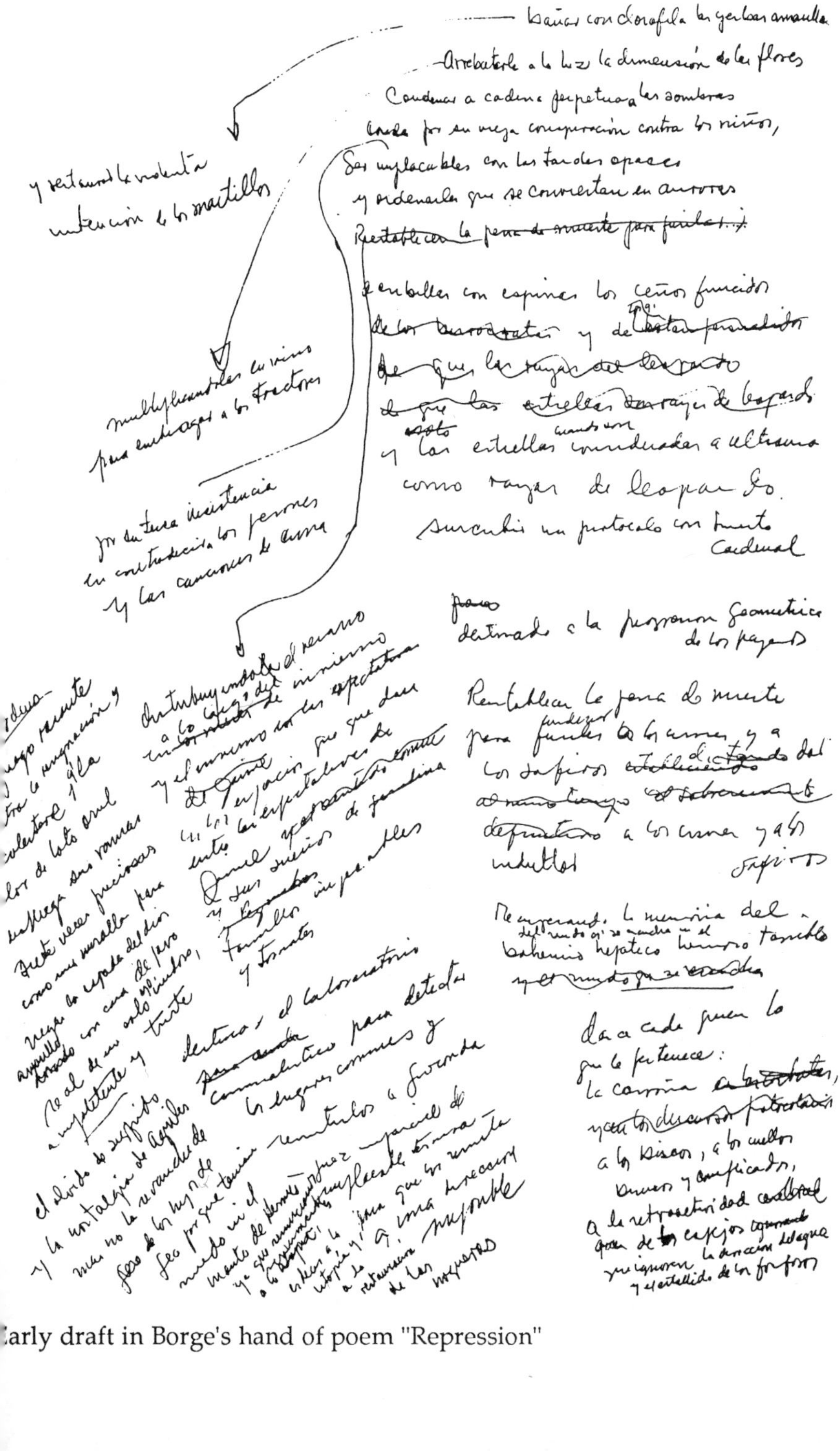
bañar con clorofila las yerbas amarillas
Arrebatarle a la luz la dimensión de las flores
Condenar a cadena perpetua a las sombras
acusadas por su vieja conspiración contra los niños,
Ser implacables con las tardes opacas
y ordenarles que se conviertan en auroras
embellecer con espinas los ceños fruncidos
~~Restablecer la pena de muerte para fusilar~~
y restaurar la violenta intención de los martillos
multiplicándoles los vinos para emborrachar a los tractores
por su terca insistencia en contradecir a las personas y las canciones de cuna
y las estrellas condenadas a ultramar como rayas de leopardo.
suscribir un protocolo con Fuente Cardenal
destinado a la progresión geométrica de los pájaros
Restablecer la pena de muerte para fusilar a los cisnes y a los zafiros

Early draft in Borge's hand of poem "Repression"

Borge with 5-year-old daughter, Valeria, February 1986

THE STORY OF MACHO MALO[1]

An Allegory for Nicaraguan Children

There was once a country called Maizgalpa,[2] rich in natural bounty, where the people cultivated poetry as well as the soil, where they caught fish in their beautiful rivers, where they captured clouds and stars in their clear sky. The people had a wise and just leader who had been born of the earth. One day their leader died and his daughter, a lovely girl named Sacuanjoche,[3] whose eyes were like two huge lakes, was left sad and all alone.

Meanwhile, in a foreign country there was a giant named Macho Malo[4] who had always wanted to possess Maizgalpa and, now that their leader was dead, desired to have Sacuanjoche. It was difficult for Macho Malo to seize Maizgalpa, because great seas and mountains protected her, as did her brave people's love for their land. There was but one secret road by which the country could be entered, and only the people of Maizgalpa knew that road. So, everyone felt confident that it would never be discovered by the terrible giant.

But unfortunately there was also in Maizgalpa a man named Satanasio.[5] He was a delinquent, a counterfeiter of money, a shiftless and ambitious fellow. While the people of Maizgalpa wished to turn their country into an enormous garden, Satanasio said this was an unrealistic dream, a dream of fools. Satanasio hated children. He insulted them, beat them up, broke their toys, and sometimes even killed them. Satanasio hated books, poetry and beauty. He was terribly viscious and egotistical. His great desire was to turn the people of Maizgalpa into slaves.

Then, one day, Satanasio went to see Macho Malo. He offered to betray his country and Sacuanjoche to the giant, asking in return that Macho Malo put him in charge. Then all the people would have to work for the benefit of the giant and Satanasio.

Satanasio showed the secret road to the hateful giant, who then took over the country. The people of Maizgalpa were turned into slaves and Sacuanjoche was locked up with seven locks and dishonored by the giant. Everyone had to work for the giant and to satisfy the appetites of Satanasio.

So that Satanasio should have no difficulty confronting the wrath and defiance of the people of Maizgalpa, Macho Malo gave him a bottle that contained a spell he could spray on them should they rebel and try to free Sacuanjoche. So it was that each time the people rebelled, Satanasio would open the bottle and the people would be left blind as though it were night. Then Satanasio's guards would go out and beat the people, killing those who stood out as leaders of the rebellion. Every year Satanasio sent Macho Malo all the riches the country had produced: cotton, coffee, gold, everything that had been produced by the people's labor.

But, in Maizgalpa there lived a boy whose name was Fearless Juan, for he was afraid of no one. Fearless Juan would steal secretly into the castle carrying flowers, poems and soothing words of encouragement for Sacuanjoche. Fearless Juan was obsessed with the idea of destroying Satanasio and, with him, the domination of Macho Malo, and of freeing Sacuanjoche. To this end, he tried to find a way to break Satanasio's evil spell.

One day he heard that in the mountains there lived a wise man with a great white beard who read and wrote books. It was said that he had found the wisest answers to people's questions about the nature of man and society. Fearless Juan went to search for this wise man. After many long days and a difficult journey, he found him. He talked with the wise man for a long time and learned much from his wisdom. Fearless Juan asked the white-bearded wise man how to break the spell by which Satanasio was able to control the people. And the wise man told Fearless Juan that the secret lay in the people organizing themselves, in struggling and turning the darkness into light. "You must turn yourself into light," the wise man told Fearless Juan.

Then Fearless Juan returned to his people and began to struggle and to organize them and to turn himself into light. He went to the mountains with a group of Satanasio's most implacable enemies and explained to them that the real enemy was the giant, Macho Malo. Each one of them would have to turn himself into light in order to dispel the darkness cast by the spell that Macho Malo had given Satanasio to dominate the people.

Fearless Juan came down from the mountains to the city spreading the secret far and wide. The number of lights grew, gradually reducing the expanse of night until the light became contagious, like a great fire. Satanasio, who had the soul of a bat, began to retreat with his guards toward a cave they had constructed, believing it to be invulnerable. And so, Satanasio was defeated. Fearless Juan's people became forever after a great light that could be seen from the farthest corners of the earth.

Now the giant, with his ferocious fangs, continues to huff and puff with rage against that awesome light, wanting to snuff it out. But what the giant doesn't know is that that old wise man with the white beard also gave Fearless Juan another secret: how to keep the light burning even in the midst of a great storm. There is no human or technological force that can snuff that light out.

THE REBIRTH OF JOSE CORONEL URTECHO

As an adolescent back in the '50s, Carlos Fonseca anticipated José Coronel Urtecho in a magazine called *Segovia,* whose editor was Francisco Buitrago. Carlos introduced various Nicaraguan poets to local Segovian readers, occasionally with illustrations by the unknown caricaturist Nieve Andino Arnesto. The understandably simple and ingenuous presentation of Coronel Urtecho by our future founder and leader — which includes a poem to Uncle Coyote that is really representative of the Vanguardist concept of folklore — stated the following:

> The extraordinary figure of José Coronel Urtecho, a Nicaraguan who writes good verses, appears as little more than a name or rank to the majority of Nicaraguans who know how to read . . .
>
> We *nornicaraguanos* are those Nicaraguans from the north who know a great deal about coffee and cattle and not much about poetry . . . To introduce José Coronel Urtecho is a literary obligation of *Segovia.* This is no military man; he is a Colonel, but only by name.[1] He was born in Granada back around 1906; he attended Jesuit school (Centroamérica) and later went on to study humanities at various universities in the United States. With the vast knowledge he acquired and his own creative talent, he was able to inspire the generation from Granada that a short time thereafter would be called the Vanguardist movement, in which flowered poets like Pablo Antonio Cuadra and Joaquín Pasos.
>
> He has been a deputy to the National Congress and represented Nicaragua at the centennial celebration of the University of Salamanca. His refuge was always the Hacienda San Francisco del Río, on the banks of Nicaragua's San Juan River. He has distinguished himself in the Western Hemisphere as the best translator of U.S. poetry, and recently, in his book *Rapid Transit,* he has described brilliantly the life

and work of the people of the United States at the time he was there studying. Through this book one comes to know San Francisco, California, the waters of the Mississippi, a little history of the San Juan River, and vague recollections in which the reader himself seems to participate in the adventure of the protagonist: Coronel Urtecho.

He has cultivated all phases of poetry. Among his popular poetic works is his "Little Ode to Uncle Coyote", especially popular for its nursery rhyme flavor:

And the critter, tooth broken
tail smokin',
drowned in the lagoon
diving for the cheese in the moon.
And there begins his glory
where ends his worry,
thus also did go
Li-Tai-Po
Chinese Poet.

His best known poetic works are: "The Parks", "Ode to Rubén", "Mombacho", and "Portrait of Thy Neighbor's Wife". In prose, short novels or *noveletas,* as he calls them, and theatrical works like *La petenera* and *Chinfonía burguesa,* which he wrote together with Joaquín Pasos. His most recent work is *Rapid Transit.* At present he resides in New York.

Ten years later, when the FSLN already existed, Carlos met José Coronel Urtecho in Managua, at the home of Napoleón Chow, where he surprised him with that famous remark: "You know, after Somoza the person most responsible for the situation in Nicaragua is you . . ."

Why this youthful interest of Carlos Fonseca's in introducing us in *Segovia* to "a Nicaraguan who writes good verses"? And why the interest of the mature political activist in conversing with that singular man, accusing him straight away and confronting him ideologically? Whatever the reasons, Carlos confirms here his sense of foresight, his frankness, and at the same time the confidence he had in José Coronel's personal integrity, so vital to the clandestine revolutionary, for the fact he sought to meet with Coronel was itself a demonstration of his faith in that integrity and of his respect for this intellectual. There is not the slightest doubt that, were he alive today, the principal founder of the FSLN would be here celebrating José Coronel's 80th birthday together with all of us, the FSLN and the revolutionary government; he would be celebrating the new birth of this great Nicaraguan poet.

Indeed, José Coronel was reborn when poetry was reborn in him and he had the lucidity — in this case political as well as moral — to recognize the volcano and accept the rainbow's invitation. One evening in May 1980, at the home of Ernesto Cardenal and in the presence of many friends, José Coronel Urtecho himself read the certificate of his new birth, which means this man who now celebrates his 80th birthday was born at age 73 or 74. His rebirth certificate, I believe, reads more or less as follows:

> After 20 years of poetic silence, or rather sterility, which I unhesitatingly confess, morally crushed under the sense of guilt suffered by much of the country, excepting the oppressed and exploited, the youth, and above all the Sandinista Front, which redeemed the country, freed it of ignominy and led it to victory, I have once again felt the irresistible need to write impersonal, objective, concrete poems that help give verbal form and graphic architecture to the immense content of Nicaragua's irreversible, invincible, incomparable revolution.

If a poet is faithful, and only if he is faithful, to his people, it is because he is an honest being, a poet faithful to poetry, a poet who lets himself direct and be directed by poetry while remaining faithful to his people, that is, poetry and the people brand you with their magnetic north and lead you to honesty. And honesty leads you to revolution. Some years ago the Nicaraguan bourgeoisie — "obese, elegant and brainless", the most exploitative class in Nicaraguan history, dependent, primitive and mentally retarded — accused José

Coronel of being a traitor; a traitor to his class, in other words, which is a great compliment.

José Coronel's 80th birthday will inevitably and rightly be the occasion for a great deal of recognition. Much will be said about him, about his abundant production of verse and prose, about his never-ending enjoyment of conversation and his invulnerable capacity for joy; he will be accused of co-responsibility for Nicaragua's magnificent literary heritage of the past fifty years. We, for our part, will refer to his primary virtue, which is, curiously, a virtue rooted in his principal sins — the virtue of having reached the highest level of decency through a constant, implacable and opportune exercise of self-criticism.

Only the elderly and the deceased are capable of self-criticism. Indeed, there are too many deceased and too many elderly, but José Coronel Urtecho, who is alive and incapable of dying, was a critic of his own class, having severely criticized both the Vanguard movement and José Coronel Urtecho himself.

From the 1930s, when he returned to Nicaragua from the United States and gathered around him a group of young intellectuals, down to his most recent poems Coronel Urtecho has devoted himself to promoting Nicaragua's erudite culture. He is the one who prompted the shift in the center of cultural production from Nicaragua's west to east coast.

As a member and protagonist of the Generation of '27, he did not escape the great crisis of the inter-war period and the post-war years, the crisis of western culture. As Matthew Arnold used to say, people of that era were between a world that had just died and one that had not yet been born. His, then, is the inter-war generation; the one that initiates the debate that can no longer be postponed about two opposing economic, political, ideological and cultural systems; the generation that suffers the impact of the first socialist revolution; the generation of the Spanish Civil War, whose defeat carries with it the blood of Miguel Hernández and Federico García Lorca. It's the generation of the Córdoba university reforms; Alejo Carpentier's generation; what would have been Carlos Mariátegui's generation. It is also the generation of Jorge Luis Borges, who was enamored of English culture and not very proud of his own American roots. It's the generation of Sandino, political precursor by whom all men of the time, without exception, were measured. It's a divided generation, predestined by history to rebel.

The Nicaraguan literary vanguard chose nature, landscapes, trees, flowers, fruits, birds, lakes and volcanoes, together with hammocks, *jícaras*[2] and *tapescos*[3] and a poor peasant and artisan people, whose speech they adopted without appropriating its class content, regurgitating it in a radically original form. José Coronel's interpretation is as follows:

> In the late '20s and early '30s there appeared among the so-called Vanguard group in Granada some young iconoclasts, or at least irreverent youths, who together with me tried to free both our speech and our lives of all bourgeois hindrances and adiposities or expressions, calling things not only by their proper names but also at times calling bread wine and wine bread, as if changing through words the very form of things, but perhaps now with the intention . . . of one day in Nicaragua changing bread into real bread and wine into real wine, not just the imported kind but also, perhaps, bread and wine produced in the country and available to everyone.[4]

They were born to politics with the name reactionaries, and they were reactionaries by virtue of their snobism and their convictions. As they used the word, it meant looking to the past for support, or as Coronel would say repeating what he thought were the words of Jean Cocteau, going with their parents alongside their grandparents. Actually, however, it corresponded to their class extraction. Their grandparents were the previous reactionaries, the ones from before, the colonial past. Coronel sneezed; he reacted against that class, his own, as when they call your mother names without your leaving her side until much later. For him business and speculation were the opposite of culture. They were the anti-culture, although he would not come to see that one had to be against the class in which the anti-culture took root as such. That's why they also declared themselves in favor of the

Somoza dictatorship. All this shows us clearly that the literary Vanguard was at once contradictory, irresponsible, brilliant and influential. Political absolution of the Vanguard literary movement is not possible, but there is no doubt that the revolutionary vanguard has forever absolved José Coronel Urtecho.

José Coronel's ideas are recorded in his written works, but in addition this poet teaches, stimulates and illustrates as he speaks. In his aesthetic ideas there is total coherence. The disrespectful José profoundly respects universal culture. Ever since his first trip to the United States he has learned from modern U.S. poetry, from the poetry of Elliot, Pound and above all William Carlos Williams.

Let us not be fooled, however, by his ingenuous face, which provides little if any clue to the seriousness with which he plays chess and enjoys culture. Behind that seemingly spontaneous and irreverent iconoclast lies a rigorous intellectual, a studious man attuned to cultural production, or at the very least an assiduous observer of the meaning and form employed by contemporary poets.

The sad self-satisfaction of a badly imitated modernism, the arrogant, unintelligible language of INCAE[5] — to which Coronel made his final ideological concessions — and the set phrases, ambiguities, romantic vagueness and pseudo-truths, the platitudes, the donkeyshit spewed out by the tyranny, its cruelty, the exploitation, the naked arrogance of foreign domination, all led to a crisis to which the only possible response was revolution, that is, the triumph of justice and freedom and the possibility of a new aesthetics.

In José Coronel's opinion the intellectuals, the poets, were the ones called upon to confront the inflation of language, making one last attempt to interest the bourgeoisie in a modern response. What he failed to detect is that by its very nature that bourgeoisie was comprised of technocrats and evil people, who were the dark ants of that verbal labyrinth.

Finally, with rare exception, it was the poets and other artists — disciples of Coronel, to be sure — who, wielding metaphors and paint brushes, assault rifles and contact bombs, did Somoza in. It is they who, identifying with the classes that made the revolutionary vanguard possible, joined in and contributed to the epilogue and to the opening of new chapters in this history that is becoming more and more a true history.

José Coronel recalled that Darío, whom he baptized with the commonplace of "Bolívar of Culture" — so as to confer upon him the rank of general in this confrontation —, was the leader of Spanish American cultural independence and the hero of national culture.

Coronel knows how the relationship between politics and intellectuals comes about and how throughout time these two fields have come together and gone their separate ways. From colonial times politics has been the only way out for the thinker, for the worker of words. Thanks to the intellectuals, he says, some words actually had meaning and even a certain reality.

Reiterating rain upon water, in the 19th century Rubén Darío is an exemplary case, for he represents the height of separation between the poet and everything else, the separation of reality from the verb and from verse, and he represents the political and economic reality of his "municipal and dense" time, as Darío himself called it.

Nevertheless, the modernist tradition that was deliberately directed to aestheticism — to the opposite side of the street from a modernism with leopard's claws, an immaculate swan in whose wings were manifest the struggles against the barbarians and the poisoned dart of Nemrod — did not take root, and the following generation, that of 1927 — Coronel's generation — marched in the opposite direction, although in '36, acting as a politician, the intellectual did not in those cruel moments achieve the stature of his words. "Life lived and shared as life of the people" is but a desire. Starting in those years he denounces the accelerated militarization and commercialization that amount, says José Coronel, to a "disintellectualization and deculturization" of the country, openly denounced by Ernesto Cardenal, who in the '40s and '50s brings word and action together.

For Coronel, giving their due to poetry and the intellectuals is above all to defend culture from the monetarist spirit of the Granada oligarchy, in the corroded sense of the word. We agree with him in this thought, but also insist on the need to go to the root, to the class itself and to confront that class, in order to make it possible for the spirit of the new revolutionary culture to exist. It's what Coronel himself would say later on when he referred to Leonel Rugama. To defend the poets, we would add, is to defend intelligence, that is, the plow, since the seed is the principles and objectives of the revolutionary classes.

For Coronel, culture is that which is born of culture itself, which changes and is transformed. Culture is a synthesis "of all knowledge relevant to the man of our time" — thesis that would be surpassed afterward, although at the time he explained it as follows:

> Culture is not a matter of possessing a great deal of knowledge, nor even less of possessing specialized scientific knowledge, rather of one's knowledge and experience forming an organic, living whole that is revealed in the activities and expressions of a person or a collectivity . . . I believe it was Max Scheller who said or quoted the saying that the cultured man is the one who if he knows, no one knows he knows, and if he doesn't know, no one knows he doesn't know.[6]

For the Revolution, culture must not be a monopoly of the intellectuals; it must not be private property. It must belong to the people, concepts José Coronel would himself eventually come to share.

But in order for this culture to exist, the air must be conditioned. It must cease to be culture in the anthropological sense and become culture in accord with the new values, that is, universal culture, for it is a culture of our reality and of our time.

It's not my place to be the Lone Ranger settling accounts with the ideological conscience of the past. From a general point of view, I think there is no doubt that the literary Vanguard movement, and therefore José Coronel, contributes artistic elements that the revolution appropriates fundamentally through Leonel Rugama. The eruption of this new politico-literary dimension occurs in the context where the struggle for culture is not separate from the struggle for revolutionary transformation. But it is indisputable that this rupture of political contexts utilized the metamorphosis of language created by the Vanguard movement.

José Coronel admits this, too. Therefore, what seems to us most worthy of recognition in our poet is his lucid decision to assume the responsibility that is his for some of the sins of our history. To conclude, it is not a rhetorical statement to say of José Coronel, as he turns eighty, what he has himself said of his wife, María: "So much life at such an age!" And this vitality that manifests itself not only in his criticism of the past, but also in his sustained and almost resplendant effort to understand the Revolution, is a kind of lucid agony, which is life and not death, to place himself in the perspective of the revolutionary people. This is reflected in his three great poems written under the sign of the popular victory: "Panels of Hell", "The Past Shall Not Return", and "Conversation With Carlos".

His fondness for cards and his continual reiteration of arguments, as well as his use of dialectics in the area of aesthetic expression, complete, or rather characterize the personality of José Coronel. But it is María Kautz who defines José Coronel's profile — this woman who is truly a woman; this woman who is simply a woman and many women at once. The conjunctions of pronouns, nouns and verbs and a few adjectives that José Coronel parades en masse through his poetry are requirements demanded by the union with his wife, who has been existence itself for the poet. "It is enough that you are here, that you are, that I can speak to you, that I call you María to know who I am and to know who you are." This is not a game of words; it is rather that the distance between this man and this woman is only what is required for him to be, even while she is. It would be unjust to speak of José Coronel without mentioning María Kautz, or to speak of María Kautz ignoring José Coronel.

Eighty years are not excessive in the life of a great poet. Should we one day discover a magic of geriatrics, a drug to prolong life indefinitely, among those who should be selected for its use — this is perhaps our own egotism, as we wish to continue enjoying his pleasure, his happiness, his terrible, geometric look, coconut nougat, so as never to be bored — should be José Coronel Urtecho.

The dullwitted and iniquitous Nicaraguan bourgeoisie rejected the offer. The Revolution made him its own from the beginning: now bread has been turned into bread, now wine has been turned into wine. Now, José Coronel, we can share wine and bread.

JULIO CORTAZAR.
COMRADE IN PRISON AND IN FREEDOM.

The Resistance, Prison and Books

As long as there is revolution on earth there will be *cronopios*,[1] for revolution is the struggle for and conquest of freedom; it procures love and the fulfillment of love; and the cronopios seek to express and embody precisely these permutations.

One day in the midst of the struggle to liberate Nicaragua, in the midst of the search for freedom and love, from within that tense and compartmented world of the resistance, I saw Julio Cortázar pass by like a deer running across the *pampas*. So Cortázar appears in me during the resistance; that is where we first met, something I suspect he himself doesn't know. It was when my companion Josefina, who was then not yet my companion, in one of those inevitable exchanges that take place between two people who will eventually become a couple, placed in my hands *The Prizes*, his first novel. An interesting image, albeit fleeting.

But where I really came to know Cortázar, or more exactly, where I first recognized him, was during my last incarceration in a Somoza prison from early 1976 until the month of August 1978, for he was in prison with me. And he doesn't know that, either. Again it was Josefina who brought Cortázar into that prison, that is, it was she who introduced me to his works: *A Manual for Manuel, Hopscotch*, and other titles. The ignorance of that herd of animals formed of the military censors, who probably were unaware of Cortázar's existence and to whom his name no doubt sounded like that of the author of Greek legends, permitted his presence. As a rule, I was allowed almost no books.

The titles of publications were decisive: if they raised any doubts they ended up in the fire; if not, they might be spared and remain in prison. On one occasion someone brought me the work of an unknown North American author: *Mental Energy*, by Orison Sweet Marden. The inquisitors, of course, wouldn't let it pass, because that "mental energy" would surely provide me with sufficient secret weapons to make my escape. They unexpectedly let George Politzer's *Elements of Philosophy* through because it had to do with philosophy, which they deemed inconsequential and inoffensive. Had someone sent me Gunter Grass's *The Tin Drum,* they would have prohibited it simply because of the word "drum", although they might have allowed it because of the word "tin".

The incredible part of this prohibition and circulation of books was the fortunate ignorance of the censors, who permitted me to have Cortázar's books, so that I really came to know and appreciate him there in prison. Moreover, he himself came and went on his own through unimagined invisible cracks. He'd slip in secretly, silently, and we would carry on frequent conversations. He was an assiduous visitor, although he didn't know it. And I began to have a friendship with Cortázar that continues to this day.

Strangely enough, despite our closeness Cortázar never proposed any plan of escape. So I never did escape, in any sense; I was always aware of my situation and of the modest contribution I was making to the revolutionary process from prison. I was tortured by loneliness, too. On one occasion Gioconda Belli sent me a reassuring note that said: "Tomás, you're not alone." Cortázar accompanied me in the same way. His imagination, his fiction, his constant construction and reconstruction of worlds, his *62/Model to Build* and *All Fires the Fire,* were company for me, a moral stimulus, and in a way even a literary incentive, for that was when I wrote the only book I've ever written, a little grouping of pages entitled *Carlos, The Dawn Is No Longer Beyond Our Reach.*

Cortázar's story about Che Guevara called "Meeting" made a great impact on me. Impressed by it and taking it as a reference point, I wrote a letter to René Núñez, a letter that, somewhere in our hurried comings and goings, between drops and safe houses, between the resistance and the final victory, disappeared. In that letter I related a story about Carlos Fonseca, which from a literary viewpoint was, in my judgment, rather successful. I have never been able to reconstruct it and were I to attempt to do so today, I would perhaps lack the same impetus and spontaneity as when I first wrote it.

Likewise, *A Manual for Manuel* constituted a political and literary stimulus. And there were, of course, the tremendous enigmas of *Hopscotch*, enigmas that even in my subsequent personal relationship with Cortázar I have not dared to clarify or decipher. I prefer that these enigmas remain intact. I read *Hopscotch* in a linear fashion, which is one of the ways to read it that Cortázar proposes in his preliminary "Table of Advice". I also read it from end to beginning and from beginning to end. It's a multilayered work; two, three, four worlds; different novels; a true piece of literature where we the readers end up being the authors. Both in prison and out the literature of Cortázar is a call to the imagination; but for me at no time was it ever an escape, an evasion of my duty and my conscience. Nothing could have been more stimulating for thinking up new revolutionary projects. The imagination, fiction, scarcely envisage, scarcely suggest the broadest outlines of reality as rendered by a revolution.

Moreover, Cortázar's style amazed me. His irony is filled with tenderness, yet does not hide its identity as irony. I would suppose it has its roots in the River Plate, but that Cortázar synthesizes it and carries it to universal and novel dimensions. He's audacious with language. Utilizing the everyday spoken language from every corner of this America of ours, the language of ordinary folk, our brother and neighbor took the literary world by storm. The result was the new Latin American literature. His audacity never loses touch with reality, nor is it lacking in content, for it seeks to create symbols and personalities that are at once admirable and intelligible: the cronopios, the sorceress, or his jazz musician.

Cortázar has influenced me in my public speaking, because I speak much and write little. I try to use irony and certain turns of phrase that have slanderously been called poetic. But our literature is oral and has to be set down in writing for other purposes, while his literature is written and, as is proper, can only be heard with the eyes and the senses. That is the difference; different procedures, yet the same. But I only knew Cortázar by his printed words; his physical appearance under the prison lamps and by what little sunlight filtered in during the day, was only printed words, the typography of his works.

An Unerring Cronopio. A Letter I Never Wrote And The Reply We Received.

When Cortázar would leave and I remained behind in prison, we would continue to communicate in some fashion. Perhaps by remote control; maybe directly through a cronopio with unerring and very clear transmissions. At the time, Cortázar was in Paris writing; in Mexico or Rome with the Bertrand Russell Tribunal; or in San José, Costa Rica; and I, isolated, protesting and skinny, was in the Tipitapa Model Prison. One day I had a desire to write him a letter, but my intentions remained unrealized. I was sure that he would reply; I was completely certain he would answer me. But I never wrote the letter.

Nevertheless, Cortázar responded. He had always responded to the needs of the Nicaraguan people. The proof was that at that very moment Cortázar signed a message expressing his solidarity and personal identity with our people's struggle under the leadership of the FSLN. That was his reply to the letter I neither wrote nor sent. I only recently read that message, which appeared in Sandinista publications and sympathetic magazines and newspapers in America and Europe. It reads as follows:

> Although widely known throughout the world, one appreciates the tragic political and social situation of the people of Nicaragua more intimately and with greater clarity when he sets foot on the soil of a neighboring country, as is the case of Costa Rica, for the firsthand accounts of that situation multiply as you meet the exiles and the relatives of innumerable victims and prisoners of the Somoza régime.
>
> That is why I do not wish to leave San José without registering my repudiation of so many endless violations of human rights and of the most elementary

laws of a democratic society. The Bertrand Russell Tribunal, of which I was a jury member and with which were associated the most eminent personalities of our time, on numerous occasions expressed its energetic condemnation of the ruling régime in Nicaragua. I feel that that condemnation must be tirelessly repeated by all who believe in democracy and freedom; I believe that the government of Nicaragua must be obliged to respect the laws and rights of man. My protest is not merely personal; I know that it embraces millions of people in Latin America and throughout the world who will never accept régimes based on hate, oppression and disdain for human values.

Julio Cortázar

Cortázar Is Larger Than His Physical Stature

In mid-October 1979, shortly after the revolutionary victory, General Omar Torrijos telephoned me from Panama offering us the opportunity to invite Cortázar to Nicaragua, since he was close enough to hear and feel our national euphoria as it spread over the Isthmus. Julio, of course, had already decided to come to Nicaragua. Torrijos and we limited ourselves to facilitating his inevitable reentry. We immediately sent an airplane, the "19 DE JULIO", to pick him up. But it turned out that a day or so prior to the arrival of our plane Cortázar had been mugged and his passport and money stolen. Torrijos, for his part, had also placed an aircraft at his disposal in order to facilitate the trip. Thus Cortázar found himself without documents and penniless, but with two airplanes fully ready to transport him, so he took off.

This was the second time he had come to Nicaragua — once before he had been clandestinely, with his lanky and thoroughly unclandestine figure, in Solentiname together with Ernesto Cardenal, the local community and Sergio Ramírez — but it was the first time he had arrived in a liberated and revolutionary Nicaragua. On that occasion I went to the airport to receive him as befits a respected and eminently honest writer, and there I had the good fortune to meet in person my old friend and prison visitor who had seemed so inoffensive to the blind eyes of the military censors and had breached the military security apparatus put in place to keep the Sandinista prisoners incommunicado. Inasmuch as I held him in great esteem, I took him and his companion Carol to my home. Ever since, Cortázar and Carol have resided in Nicaragua; they've left and come back and always stay and live among us, returning to our homes. Cortázar circles the day in eighty worlds and stops, descends, lands in Nicaragua, and continues on to his beloved Buenos Aires. Although his address and postal box are in Paris, Cortázar is a Latin American and has never ceased being one; that is, he's never stopped experiencing the pleasure and suffering of being Latin American: the banishments and struggles, the pains and hopes. Perhaps his trips to Nicaragua have reinvigorated his roots and have grounded him more firmly in this new piece of free territory, a prelude of the entire continent.

Carol and Josefina have become fast friends, our house is their house, we share my home and many hours of conversation. When Cortázar is here, I interrupt my work as much as I can to be with him, and invariably I find him writing, reading, expressing interest in those around him. He refuses no phone call, nor denies anyone an interview.

Cortázar discovers Nicaragua each time he comes. He wants to see all of it. He's here, there and everywhere: among the people, at the volcanoes, on the rivers, on the Atlantic Coast, visiting cooperatives, with the literacy program (which he called tenderly and fantastically "The Battle of the Pencils"), at cultural activities. He knows no fatigue, continuing to support the Museum of Latin American Art in solidarity with Nicaragua, making statements, countering the lies of the pro-imperialist news transnationals in Europe, drafting documents, seeking signatures for and signing communiques in support of Nicaragua, Guatemala, El Salvador and his native Argentina. He comes and goes clandestinely, as when he slipped through the bars of the Somoza tyranny; he enters Argentina and searches for his childhood in order to evoke Darío's "Colloquium of the

Centaurs" (one cannot have Argentine and Latin American roots and not take into account Rubén Darío); he gives readings in the patio of the ASTC's "Casa Fernando Gordillo"; he inaugurates the Ministry of Culture's "Poetry Tuesdays"; he drinks Flor de Caña rum with his friends; he stands vigil on the northern frontier with progressive intellectuals from the United States; he receives the Rubén Darío Order of Cultural Independence; and he defends our threatened and besieged Sandinista People's Revolution.

Cortázar recently suffered a personal tragedy and I was fearful of his return. He would now be coming without Carol and our house, my *compañera,* the familial ambiance, the landscape might all prove disagreeable to him; they might injure his sensibilities. But he reappeared and I saw the same old Cortázar, rising above his pain and transcending it. The explanation, we felt, was that his love itself consoled him. When one has truely known how to love, there is no guilt complex. While it may seem a contradiction, he who is capable of love suffers the loss of a loved one less than the person who has been unable to show or demonstrate sufficient love.

Pain is sometimes accompanied by remorse. The loss of a human being hurts in large measure because of guilt complexes that don't exist when someone like Cortázar has been able to love his companion in an integral way; which also reflects Cortázar's capacity for commitment to others. In such situations, people like Cortázar are less vulnerable than those who give nothing of themselves. They don't feel the impact of pain as much. Love alleviates our pain and defends us from death.

One night Carol asked to speak with me alone. She had severe pain in her bones. With hands full of mystery and blue eyes she communicated to me the secret that she had only a few months to live. What moved me, and moved me all the more when her secret was revealed by its own drama, were her words: "I wish Julio might die first so that he could be spared the pain of my death." When Claribel Alegría communicated the news of Carol's death to me, I became aware of the magnitude of that great love.

Perhaps the synthesis of our entire relationship — maybe even the synthesis of Cortázar himself — is that each time he has come and gone and I have accompanied him to the airport to see him off, I have thought of him less and less as the celebrated author of *Hopscotch, A Manual for Manuel,* "Meeting", or *The Prizes.* The famous writer has gradually vanished before my eyes; erased himself to become simply a beautiful human being. He even appears physically shorter to me as compared to his human and moral stature.

Cortázar is so large, so tall as a person, so humanly profound, that he is able to make himself smaller and to diminish his fame in order to move through life, through the streets, with the same stature as ordinary folks. Cortázar is the size of a man, which is to say, he's taller than his actual height. Next to him I don't feel like a runt, nor do I feel like the simple reader of his works and of literature that I've been, rather I feel as though I'm in the company of my brother. He's an individual in whom simplicity, tenderness and modesty coexist naturally and openly.

Yet I feel he is unaware of his unpretentiousness; he's unaware that he is a modest man, although he probably has some notion of his tenderness. All of us who know him are quite conscious of these qualities. Cortázar's stature goes beyond his physical height and extends beyond his literature.

I have noted a series of virtues in Cortázar which, insofar as possible, I have tried to cultivate in myself, if indeed I possess any at all. I would like to be like Cortázar, but not as a writer, rather as a human being. I would like to grow as a man, even if it were not possible for me to become an artist. And while it certainly is true that I could never aspire to be a writer like Julio, I do have the right and the obligation to be a man like Julio.

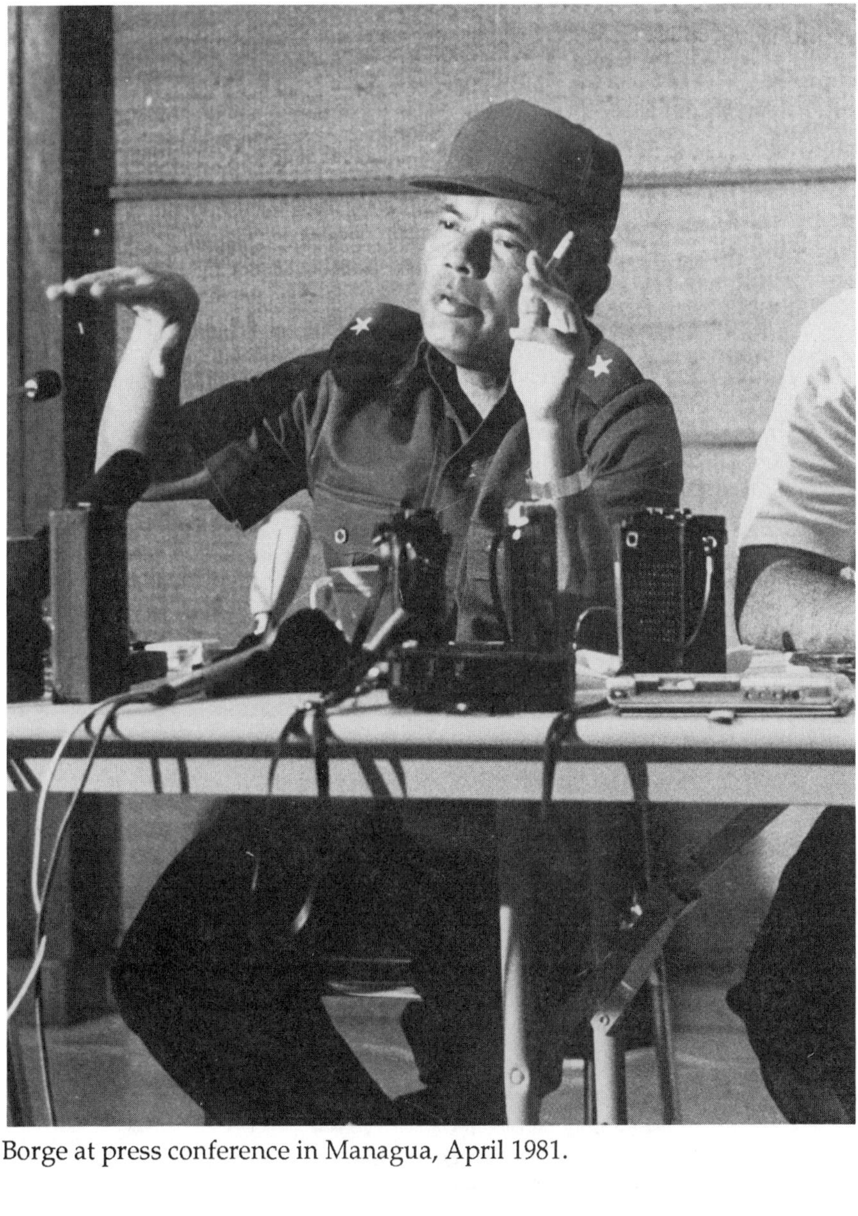

Borge at press conference in Managua, April 1981.

NOTES

CREATIVITY IN THE REVOLUTION: THE LITERARY BORGE

1. Margaret Randall, interview, Managua, 16 January 1982.

2. The thoroughly transparent attempts by the Reagan Administration to link Sandinista and Cuban leaders to international narcotics trafficking only highlights the deviousness of domestic disinformation within the United States. Even as the President proclaimed on national television: "I know that all American parents who are concerned about the drug problem will be enraged to hear that high-ranking members of the Nicaraguan government are deeply involved in drug trafficking," both the Drug Enforcement Administration and the Central Intelligence Agency denied that there was any credible evidence to support such allegations. Indeed, the evidence is now overwhelming that since the 1950s successive U.S. Administrations have aided and abetted international drug traffickers in the pursuit of foreign policy objectives and that the Reagan Administration has been particularly hypocritical in the utilization of drug money for political ends in Central America. Three major PBS broadcasts, for example, have presented some of this evidence to national television audiences: Bill Moyer's "The Secret Government . . . The Constitution in Crisis", aired on 4 November 1987; a "Frontline" program on 19 April 1988 entitled "Murder on the Rio San Juan"; and a Documentary by former CBS News producer Leslie Cockburn titled "Guns, Drugs, and the CIA", also broadcast by "Frontline" on 17 May 1988.

Pertinent print sources in the public domain include: Leslie Cockburn, *Out of Control* (NY: Atlantic Monthly Press, 1987); *Covert Action Information Bulletin*, No. 28 (Summer 1987): 13-18; *Newsweek* (12 October 1987): 36; Jonathan Kwitny, *The Crimes of Patriots* (NY and London: Norton, 1987); United States District Court, Southern District of Florida, Civil Action No. 86-1146-CIV-KING, Tony Avirgan and Martha Honey, plaintiffs, vs. John Hull, Rene Corbo, etc. *Declaration of Plaintiffs' Counsel* (Christic Institute, Washington, D.C.), p. 300.

3. For additional material about Borge in English, see Andrew Reding (ed.), *Christianity and Revolution. Tomás Borge's Theology of Life* (NY: Orbis, 1987); and Philip Zwerling and Connie Martin, *Nicaragua — A New Kind of Revolution* (Westport: Lawrence Hill, 1987), pp, 206-213.

4. Zwerling and Martin, *op. cit.*, p. 206.

5. Anastasio Somoza García, founder of the family dynasty that would rule Nicaragua for four and a half decades, notes Stan Persky,

"was a man of dubious but perhaps appropriate talents." He studied at the Pierce School of Business in Philadelphia, after which "he became an unsuccessful automobile dealer in Nicaragua, followed by a brief stint as a health officer for the Rockefeller Foundation." By virtue of personal charm and his knowledge of English gained in Philadelphia, Somoza García ingratiated himself with Ambassador Matthew Hanna and the U.S. Marines, who appointed him head of Nicaragua's U.S.-created National Guard before the American occupation forces were withdrawn in 1933. "Behind the guns of the National Guard," writes Persky, "he bought *haciendas* from political opponents at cut-rate prices. The country's public works program consisted of improving his properties and building roads to them. Within three years of assuming office, his fortune amounted to $3 million, a sizable sum in the midst of the Depression." See Persky, *America, the Last Domino* (Vancouver: New Star, 1984), p. 202.

Somoza García, adds Gregorio Selser, returned from his stay in the United States without having completed his studies, but with a well-established reputation "as a gambler, playboy, dancer and womanizer." He had served a brief jail term in Philadelphia for counterfeiting and now, back in Nicaragua, quickly squandered a wholesale business his father had given him as a wedding present. His position as a "health officer", Selser clarifies, consisted of "inspecting toilets to ascertain whether or not citizens had doused them with kerosene as required to combat malaria and yellow fever." Because of the long pocket light he carried for this purpose, which suggested an officer's staff, he was dubbed "the toilet marshall". See Selser, *Nicaragua. De Walker a Somoza* (México, D.F.: Mex-Sur, 1984), pp. 229-231.

6. Tomás Borge, interview, Managua, 13 January 1982.

7. "La paciente impaciencia de Carlos," unpublished draft of Borge's memoirs, ff. 9-10.

8. Zwerling and Martin, *op. cit.*, p. 207.

9. Borge, interview, 13 January 1982.

10. "La paciente impaciencia de Carlos," ff. 1-2. Karl Friedrich May (1842-1912) was a gifted German Writer of travel and adventure stories about lands and places he was himself unable to visit. May's works are remarkable for their authenticity and the richness of detail their author was able to achieve without benefit of direct personal experience. They are characterized by an abiding sympathy for the underdog, as well as a keen appreciation of human foibles. May, observed one German critic, "neither goes along with class hatred nor with international power politics, but preaches love of one's neighbor, a sense of brotherhood by all toward all . . . He does not come to the

defense of free enterprise and of imperialism, of wealth and individual power with its corruptive effects: the nations' competitive struggle for the acquisition of raw materials, for market outlets, for spheres of influence . . . He teaches us to exchange all goods of heaven and earth in the spirit of helping and nurturing each other." See Ludwig Gurlitt, *Gerechtigkeit für Karl May!* (Radebeul, 1919), p. 139. For the story of Winnetou, see May, *Winnetou,* translated by Michael Shaw (NY: The Seabury Press, 1977).

11. Zwerling and Martin, *op. cit.,* p. 208.

12. Julio Cortázar, *Nicaragua tan violentamente dulce* (Managua: Editorial Nueva Nicaragua, 1983), p. 30.

13. See Rubén Darío, *Antología poética* (Managua: Comisión Nacional para la Celebración del Centenario del Nacimiento de Rubén Darío, 1967), pp. 243-248.

14. Modesto (Henry Ruiz) to Hermano Lobo (Tomás Borge), La Montaña, 13 July 1977. From the personal papers of Tomás Borge.

15. "Exteriorist" poetry, explains one of its principal practitioners, Fr. Ernesto Cardenal, is made "of the images of the external world, the world which is seen and palpable . . . *Exteriorismo* is objective poetry: narrative and anecdotal, made with the elements of real life and with what is concrete, with personal names and precise details, exact occurrences and numbers, facts and statements. In sum, it is a poetry of the 'Impure'." See Cardenal's introduction to *Poesía nicaragüense* (Managua, 1975).

16. Russell H. Bartley, "La poesía del comandante Tomás Borge Martínez," *Sábado,* cultural supplement to *Unomásuno* (Mexico City, 12 December 1987): 2.

STORY NUMBER TWO

1. This story was written in 1955 and first published in September 1959 in *Cuadernos Universitarios* (León, Nicaragua). Judging by its title, there may have been at least one other story, although none has been located. It was republished in the February 24, 1985 issue of *Nuevo Amanecer Cultural,* cultural supplement of the Managua daily *El Nuevo Diario.*

2. ". . . this place is definitely a shit house . . . Very interesting that novel by Jack London . . . But today I'm definitely changing my plan and going to class."

3. The holder of a secondary or high school diploma.

4. "Courage, my dear guy."

5. "Definitely, my friend."

CLANDESTINE POEMS AND PROSE

1. Published in an expanded version in *La Prensa Literaria,* 16 December 1979, together with the following poems. Adapted here for the English speaking reader.

2. Tomás Borge, *Carlos, The Dawn Is No Longer Beyond Our Reach.* Translated with introduction by Margaret Randall. Vancouver, Canada: New Star Books, 1984.

3. *Doña Bárbara* (1929): an allegorical novel of forced symbolism about good and evil, light and darkness, civilization and barbarity, by Venezuelan writer Rómulo Gallegos; *Don Segundo Sombra* (1926): an allegorical novel of marked symbolism about the disappearance of a way of life, by Argentine writer Ricardo Güiraldes.

4. *Cien años de soledad* (1967): an allegorical rendering of Latin American history by Colombian writer Gabriel García Márquez, who, drawing on his own life experience, creates a mythical universe that wins for him a prominent place in the post-war *boom* of Latin American fiction.

5. Salomón de la Silva (Nicaragua, 1893-1959).

6. "Retrato de la mujer de tu prójimo", in: José Coronel Urtecho, *Pól-la-anánta, katánta, paránta. Imitaciones y traducciones* (León, Nicaragua: Universidad Nacional Autónoma de Nicaragua, 1970), pp. 98-105.

7. Francisco Valle, *Laberinto de espadas,* (Managua: Tip. Morgantheler, 1974).

8. "Creationist" here refers to a poetic movement against *modernista* modalities that emerged in Europe at the close of the first world war and subsequently influenced poets on both sides of the Atlantic. Its origin has been attributed to Chilean poet Vicente Huidobro (1893-1948), who was a contemporary of Argentine writer Jorge Luis Borges (1899-1987) and Peruvian poet César Vallejo (1892-1938). Like Huidobro, Borges and Vallejo were affected, albeit differently, by developments in inter-war Europe; both, in their turn, have influenced Tomás Borge.

9. Joaquín Pasos (Nicaragua, 1914-1947).

10. Ramón Gómez de la Serna (Spain, 1888-1963).

11. Mariana Sansón Argüello (b. 1918, León, Nicaragua).

12. See Guillaume Apollinaire, *Oeuvres poétiques* (N.p.: Librairie Gallimard, 1956).

13. See Coronel Urtecho, *Pól-la anánta, katánta, paránta,* pp. 159-164.

14. A suggestive reference to Walt Whitman's "O Captain! My Captain!" which associates Borge with Abraham Lincoln, at the same time as it contrasts the two men's respective destinies: whereas

Lincoln's "fearful trip is done", Borge's "terrible journey" has only begun. Nor is it immediately apparent to which journey Martínez Rivas here refers: whether to that of the liberated poet who must henceforth speak in his own name, or to the precarious voyage of the revolutionary who captains an uncertain historical process; or perhaps to both at once, since they are quite inseparable.

15. In his thoroughly original manner, Borge here recaptures the quality and mood of Prévert's well-known poem "Barbara", written to commemorate "all cities destroyed by war . . . and the memory of all lovers parted by war." See Jacques Prévert, *Anthologie Prévert.* Edited by Christine Mortelier (London: Methuen Educational Ltd., 1981), p. 146.

16. Reminiscent of César Vallejo: "Me moriré en París con aguacero/un día del cual tengo ya recuerdo" (I will die in Paris with a downpour/one day I already recall). From Vallejo's "Piedra negra sobre una piedra blanca", in*Poemas humanos* (1939).

FROM THE MODEL PRISON

1. This account of Borge's imprisonment was written surreptitiously by Borge in the months following his trial and conviction in early 1977. It was smuggled out of the Model Prison where he was being held and sent to the editor of *La Prensa Literaria,* the poet Pablo Antonio Cuadra.

2. BECAT refers to the Special Brigades Against Terrorist Acts that operated within Somoza's National Guard.

PRISON POEMS AND OTHER POETRY

1. The most renowned of Sandino's officers; deceived and murdered by Somoza agents in 1937. Pedrón is a derogatory form of Pedro.

2. Andrés Castro, who in 1856 fought against the invading forces of William Walker. According to local legend, when his rifle misfired he picked up a stone and with it killed one of Walker's mercenaries.

3. Refers to divisions within the FSLN over how best to conduct the struggle against the Somoza tyranny.

4. A prescient reference to the tactical retreat of 27 June 1979, in which some 6,000 Sandinistas and armed supporters withdrew from Managua to Masaya preparatory to the final overthrow of the Somoza dictatorship. The poem also alludes to the cobblestone before it played its decisive role as the preferred building material for

barricades against the Somoza forces. Likewise, reference to Monimbó anticipates by almost six months the revolt of that famous town's indigenous population against the National Guard. Because of these elements, Borge considered titling this poem "Premonition".

5. Daughter born in 1981.

6. Borge recounts that this poem came to him in a dream.

7. Jaime Wheelock Román, Nicaraguan Minister of Agriculture and member of the National Directorate of the FSLN.

THE STORY OF MACHO MALO

1. From a speech delivered on the fourth anniversary of the death of Luis Alfonso Velásquez, a Nicaraguan youth murdered by a Somoza guardsman on 27 April 1979, and whose name now consecrates Nicaraguan places and institutions devoted to children. The full speech has been published in an illustrated children's edition: Tomás Borge, *La historia de Maizgalpa.* Ilustraciones de Roberto Zúñiga L. y Ernesto Chamorro (Tito). Managua: Asociación de Niños Sandinistas Luis Alfonso Velásquez, 1987.

2. Maizgalpa — root is *maíz* (corn), a traditional staple of the Nicaraguan diet that was gradually replaced with imported wheat as a consequence of U.S. domination; growing dependency on wheat increased Nicaragua's dependency on the United States; accordingly, a return to corn is viewed as a natural step in the larger struggle for Nicaraguan independence. The allegorical name Maizgalpa, whose ending suggests actual place names as well as the country's indigenous roots, thus alludes to the essential Nicaragua and to the constellation of elements on which true sovereignty and national dignity must rest.

3. Sacuanjoche — Nicaragua's national flower.

4. Macho Malo — literally "Bad Macho"; associates evil with machismo, or male domination, a major ill of Nicaraguan society which the Sandinista Revolution is committed to combating.

5. Satanasio — a combination of Satan and Anastasio, alluding to the satanic nature of former Nicaraguan dictator, Anastasio Somoza Debayle.

THE REBIRTH OF JOSE CORONEL URTECHO

1. A play on the Spanish word *coronel,* which means "colonel" in English.

2. Gourd receptacles typical of the Nicaraguan countryside.

3. Wall-less, flat-roofed structures of primitive construction typical of the Nicaraguan countryside.

4. *Tres conferencias a la empresa privada, y epílogo en memoria de Joaquin Zavala Urtecho* (N.p.: Ediciones El Pez y La Serpiente, 1974), p. 19.

5. Instituto Centroamericano de Administración de Empresas/ Central American Institute of Business Administration (Managua).

6. *Tres conferencias a la empresa privada,* p. 73.

JULIO CORTAZAR. COMRADE IN PRISON AND IN FREEDOM.

1. *Cronopio* is Cortázar's allegorical personification of the free spirit, unfettered by the dehumanizing conventions of social alienation or the formal constraints of language. See Julio Cortázar, *Cronopios and Famas.* Translated by Paul Blackburn. NY: Pantheon, 1969.